lauren child

My wobbly tooth must NOT ever NEVER fall out

Grosset & Dunlap

Charlie and Lola™

Text based on script written by Samantha Hill

Illustrations from the TV animation

produced by Tiger Aspect

GROSSET & DUNLAP
Published by the Penguin Group
Penguin Group (USA) Inc., 375 Hudson Street, New York, New York 10014, U.S.A.
Penguin Group (Canada), 90 Eglinton Avenue East, Suite 700, Toronto, Ontario, Canada M4P 2Y3
(a division of Pearson Penguin Canada Inc.)
Penguin Books Ltd, 80 Strand, London WC2R 0RL, England
Penguin Ireland, 25 St Stephen's Green, Dublin 2, Ireland
(a division of Penguin Books Ltd)
Penguin Group (Australia), 250 Camberwell Road, Camberwell, Victoria 3124, Australia
(a division of Pearson Australia Group Pty Ltd)
Penguin Books India Pvt Ltd, 11 Community Centre, Panchsheel Park, New Delhi - 110 017, India
Penguin Group (NZ), Cnr Airborne and Rosedale Roads, Albany, Auckland 1310, New Zealand
(a division of Pearson New Zealand Ltd)
Penguin Books (South Africa) (Pty) Ltd, 24 Sturdee Avenue, Rosebank, Johannesburg 2196, South Africa

Penguin Books Ltd, Registered Offices:
80 Strand, London WC2R 0RL, England

First published in Great Britain 2006 by Puffin Books.
Text and illustrations copyright © Lauren Child/Tiger Aspect Productions Limited, 2006
The Charlie and Lola logo is a trademark of Lauren Child. All rights reserved.
First published in the United States 2006 by Grosset & Dunlap, a division of Penguin Young Readers Group, 345 Hudson Street, New York, New York 10014. GROSSET & DUNLAP is a trademark of Penguin Group (USA) Inc. Manufactured in China.

ISBN 978-0-448-44255-6   10 9 8 7 6 5 4 3

I have this little sister, Lola.
She is small and very funny.
This week she got her
first ever wobbly tooth.

Lola says,
    "I do not ever NEVER want
my **wobbly tooth** to fall out.
    I **need** it."

Marv says, "When I had my first **wobbly tooth**,
        I nearly swallowed it.
    Luckily I was eating a toffee . . .
            and my **tooth** got stuck in it!"

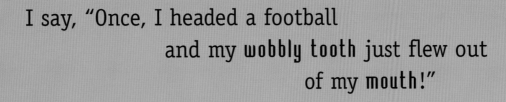

I say, "Once, I headed a football
and my wobbly tooth just flew out
of my mouth!"

"But I do not ever NEVER
want my wobbly tooth
to fall out," says Lola.

Marv says, "Why not?"

"I just **need** to keep completely
         all my **teeth**," says Lola.

And I say, "Those are just your **baby teeth**
         and they are meant to
get **wobbly** and **fall out**.
Then you will get **new teeth**—and
         they are your **grown-up** ones."

"It's like mooses," says Marv. "Mooses' antlers
fall off and then they get new ones that are
better and stronger."

"But I am not a moose!
And I like my teeth completely
the way they are . . . wobbly," says Lola.

Later Lotta comes over to play with Lola.

"Hello, everybody,
        hello, Lola. Look!"

Lola says,
"What is it, Lotta? What is it?"
And Lotta says,
        "My wobbly tooth fell out!"

"What did you get?"
says Marv.

"What do you **mean**, what did you **get**?" says Lola.
And Lotta says,
"Well, the **tooth fairy** came and . . ."
"Who is the **tooth fairy**?!" says Lola.

"Well, the tooth fairy is the tooth fairy . . .
I put my wobbly tooth under my pillow,
and then in the middle of the night
the tooth fairy came and she swapped it
for a coin," says Lotta.
"And in the morning
I bought this for
the farm.
It's a
chicken!"

Lola says,

"I didn't know there was a special fairy who gives you things when your teeth fall out! Why didn't somebody tell me this before? Nobody told me about the tooth fairy!

"My wobbly tooth must absolutely, completely come out! Now!"

Lotta says, "What will you get with your tooth money?
We need a horse and a sheep . . . and a cow."

And Lola says,
      "I'm going to get
         a giraffe."

"Do you get giraffes on a farm?"
says Lotta.

And Lola says,
"Yes, you absolutely do, Lotta . . .

"... but how do I get my wobbly tooth to fall out?"

And Lotta says, "You have to keep wobbling it."

Lola says, "I think it's almost nearly
about to come out ..."

And Lotta says,
"Just keep wobbling it."

Marv says,
"Do you want me to twist it?"
"No, Marv!" says Lola. "Mum said
absolutely no twisting, not never!"
And I say, "Keep wobbling, Lola."

"I am **wobbling** it," she says, "but it's still not coming **out**.

I don't think it's **ever** going to **come out**."

Then she squeals,
"Aaagh! Charlie . . .

It's out!
My wobbly tooth
is completely out!
And now I can get my giraffe!"

Lotta says,
  "Remember to put it under your pillow.
    You must go to bed early,
        and you must fall asleep quickly,
  or the tooth fairy will not come."

Lola says, "Yes. I'll look after
        my tooth extra carefully till bedtime,
            because I really want
                my giraffe."

"When you come over tomorrow," says Lola,
"I'll have my giraffe and you can
bring your chicken . . ."

". . . and they can be friends," says Lotta.
"Don't forget your tooth has to be
in the very, very middle of
under the pillow!"

At bedtime Lola says,
    "Charlie, I'm just going to go and
wash my tooth and make it shiny
        and clean.
            And then I . . .

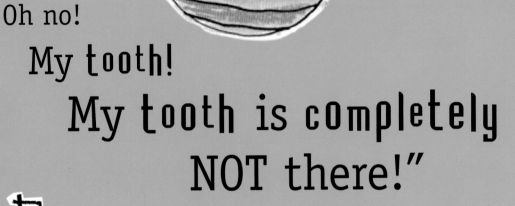

Oh no!
My tooth!
My tooth is completely
NOT there!"

I say,
"Check again.
It must be there!"

But Lola says,
"It's completely gone,
Charlie!
My tooth is
completely
NOT
there!"

I say,
"It must be somewhere!"

So we
start
searching
everywhere.

We look in the sink,

and

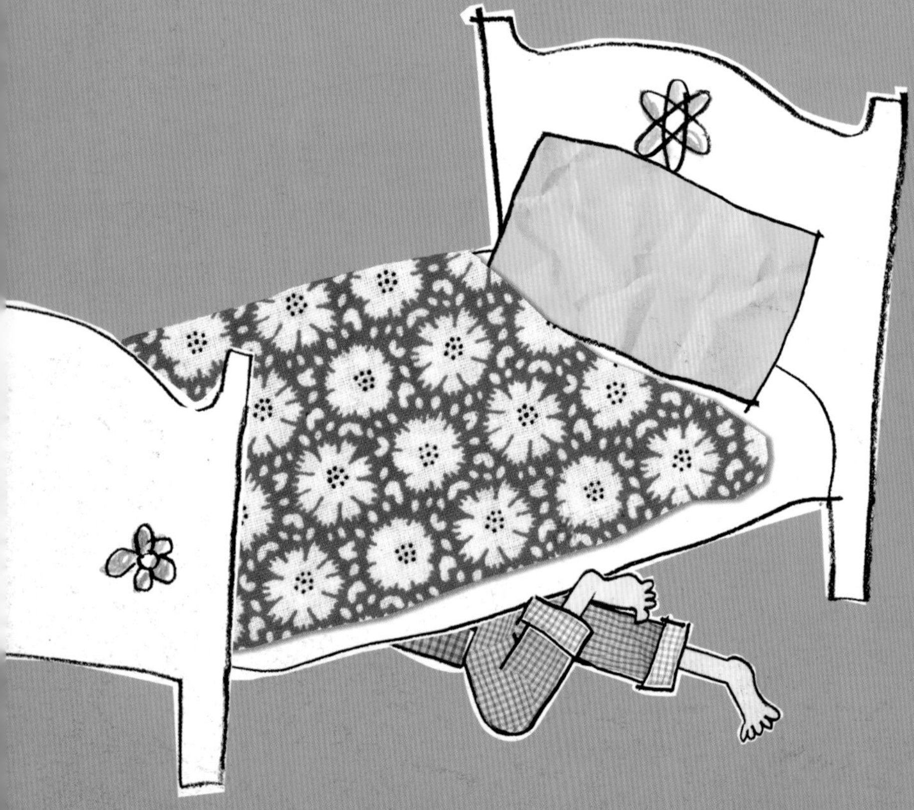

under
the

beds,

on the floor,

and

around the sofa.

Everywhere.

Then I have a really good idea.

"If you go to sleep and dream really
happy dreams tonight, you will smile.
And then the tooth fairy will see
the gap in your teeth, and she'll
know you really did honestly
lose your tooth!"

So Lola goes to bed.

"Dream really happy dreams.
Really happy dreams. Really happy . . ."

In the morning
Lola looks **under** the very
middle of her pillow.

She says,

"Charlie! The **tooth fairy** did come!
Look! Hurry up, Charlie,
I need to get a **giraffe!**"

When Lotta comes to play with Lola she says,
   "What is your giraffe called?"
Lola says, "He is called Giraffe.
      What is your chicken called?"
   Lotta says, "She's called Chicken! Hello, Giraffe."
      "Hello, Chicken. Oh look!
   I think they're friends," says Lola.

Lola says, "Maybe Giraffe and Chicken
would like to meet Mr. Goat?"
"But we don't have a goat," says Lotta.
"Oh no!" says Lola, "we don't have a goat!
We need more wobbly teeth!
Have you got any more wobbly teeth?"

Lotta says, "No. Have you?"
"I don't know," says Lola. "Is this one wobbly?"
"No," says Lotta.
Lola says, "What about . . . this one?
   Or this one? Or this one? Or this one . . ."

the Weekend Crafter

Painting
Floorcloths

20 Canvas Rugs to Stamp, Stencil, Sponge, & Spatter in a Weekend

KATHY COOPER

LARK BOOKS

ASHEVILLE, NORTH CAROLINA

EDITOR:
DEBORAH MORGENTHAL

ART DIRECTOR:
KATHLEEN HOLMES

PRODUCTION:
KATHLEEN HOLMES AND
HANNES CHAREN

ASSISTANT EDITOR:
HEATHER SMITH

PHOTOGRAPHY:
EVAN BRACKEN

Floorcloths on title page spread

Top left: **Rhonda Kaplan**, detail, *Stars and Fish*, photo by Jay Friedlander; bottom left: **Kathy Cooper**, detail, *Sunflowers and Swirls*, photo by Doyle Bussey; top right: **Joyce Garlick**, *Red Berries*, photo by Rich-Stele Prolab; bottom right: **Joyce Garlick**, *Blue Diamonds*, photo by Rich-Stele Prolab

This book is dedicated to my students.

I start each class with the following introduction (each of us fills in the blank with our own answers). These are mine:

I spend a good portion of each day
　　　--- *painting floorcloths.*
I like doing it because I'm really good at
　　　--- *playing with colors.*
In my next life I'm going to
　　　　　--- I usually say that in my next life I want *to be a singer*, but, truthfully, *I can't think of anything I'd rather do than paint floorcloths— playing with colors and singing along to music on the radio.*

Library of Congress Cataloging-in-Publication Data
Cooper, Kathy
　　Painting floorcloths : 20 canvas rugs to stamp, stencil, sponge, and spatter in a weekend / Kathy Cooper. —1st ed.
　　　　p.　cm. — (the weekend crafter)
　　Includes index.
　　ISBN 1-57990-134-4 (pbk.)
　　1. Painting　2. Floor coverings.　3. Stencil work　4. Rubber stamp printing.　I. Title.　II. Series.
　　TT385.C674　1999
　　746.6—dc21　　　　　　　　　　　　　　99-25458
　　　　　　　　　　　　　　　　　　　　　　　CIP

10 9 8 7 6 5 4 3 2 1

First Edition

Published by Lark Books
50 College St.
Asheville, NC 28801, US

©1999, Kathy Cooper

For information about distribution in the U.S., Canada, the U.K., Europe, and Asia, call Lark Books at 828-253-0467.

Distributed in Australia by Capricorn Link (Australia) Pty Ltd., P.O. Box 6651, Baulkham Hills Business Centre, NSW 2153, Australia

Printed in China by L. Rex Printing Company, Ltd.
All rights reserved
ISBN 1-57990-134-4

CONTENTS

INTRODUCTION

A LONG TIME AGO in an old house in Maine, I found a piece of preprimed canvas in my studio and became inspired to do something with it. I was looking at the bare, hardwood floors, and suddenly I remembered seeing an article about painted floorcloths. Without much painting experience, and with very little knowledge of floorcloths, I plunged in and quickly painted my first floorcloth. I was hooked.

An antiques store down the road was interested in showing a few of my early floorcloths, and within the week I had a check from my first sale. I remember thinking, this is fun, so I went to Boston and bought more canvas. Shortly after that I met a shop owner from New York City who wanted my work for her new Madison Avenue store, and she handed me a check, and told me to paint whatever I wanted to. This floorcloths thing was getting better by the minute! For me, floorcloths had become a wonderful form of self-expression, one in which I could quickly think out my ideas and see results.

After making and selling floorcloths for years, I started teaching workshops. I always learn something new from my students. This book is the result of their interest and desire to make floorclothes themselves. I have a wonderful collection of photographs showing students at the end of the weekend holding up (with great pride and huge smiles) their finished floorcloths. My students will tell you that this is something anyone can do, and then enjoy in their homes for many years.

The directions in this book are the easiest you'll find, and the information is thorough and timely. You'll learn all the basics—from hemming the canvas to transferring a design. All the simple painting techniques you'll be using in the book are described. Then you'll browse through the 20 projects, designed by me and other floorcloth artists. I'm sure you'll find several you'll want to make. To inspire you to make your own floorcloth designs, we've also included other gorgeous canvas rugs painted by these talented floorcloth artists.

A painting that you can walk on, surely you must be crazy!

Everybody asks, Can you really walk on it? It may sound strange but painted floorcloths wear like iron. A floorcloth is a water resistant rug that is somewhat flexible and will conform to the surface of the floor. Although they're made of simple materials—canvas, paints and sealant—a well-constructed floorcloth will provide years of pleasure, and hold up to substantial use. They require little special care; simply damp mop with mild soapy water when dirty, and add an occasional application of paste wax to protect the varnish.

Kathy Cooper, *Combed Checkerboard*, 3½ ' x 9½ ' (1 x 3 m). Photo by Doyle Bussey

With vinyl or linoleum available why choose a floorcloth?

In a way, floorcloths are like vinyl flooring except that they're painted and made to be used as an accent rug. In fact long before we had linoleum or vinyl we had floorcloths. They were popular for the same reasons we loved linoleum and then vinyl—they could be wiped clean. But the truly great thing about a floorcloth is that you can coordinate the design and the colors to go in your own space, whether it's a small rug in front of the sink or a large canvas under your dining room table. Unlike a woven rug, a floorcloth is easily cleaned with a damp mop—and it's allergy free!

Do I need a big space to paint in? Are they hard to make? Do they take a lot of time?

Making a floorcloth today is much easier and quicker than you might think. And you don't need a lot of space. Today we have the advantage of wonderful fast-drying, easy-to-use acrylic paints, and preprimed canvas that is ready to paint on. You'll find most of the materials you need at your local art- or craft-supply store. Find a place in your house where you can spread out and paint. The basement floor or the dining room table both work fine.

I've never painted anything before! How do I know if I can paint a floorcloth?

One of the greatest joys in a floorcloth workshop is to watch nonpainters turn into painters—in a weekend! Initially my students hold the brushes timidly, a worried look on their face. Then we just plunge in and start painting, and in a few minutes they're hooked! They have paint under their nails, in their hair and on their clothes, and they look a lot like happy kids in kindergarten. Remember how much you loved finger painting? The painting techniques used in these projects are all easy to do. You don't need any sophisticated painting skills to achieve great-looking results. Simple designs can produce elegant floorcloths. In fact, some early floorcloths were painted in one solid color.

I have a place in my home where I'd like to put a floorcloth. How do I decide which one to make?

The first thing I tell people trying to decide on a floorcloth is to decide where they want to use it. A floorcloth is a great solution for many rooms, but not perfect for every room. Select a space where you might like to add a splash of color. The space needs to have a firm floor, such as hardwood or vinyl instead of carpet. A floorcloth can be used over a low rigid carpet but doesn't work well over plush pile since there is so much give under the weight of your foot.

Once you've decided where you'll use the floorcloth, you can give some thought to the size and colors which will work in that space. Most of the designs in this book could be adapted to other size rugs with some adjustment to the measurements of the design. All of these projects could be executed in other colors of your choice. Put a few fabric or wallpaper scraps from your space in an envelope when you go the craft-supply store, and select your colors to blend with what you already have.

I have a hard time making decisions about design choices and color. Help me out here.

Take a good look at the space where you plan to put your floorcloth. You might even have a photograph of the space. Look at what your eye is drawn to. Does your room need a colorful accent or something subtle

Kathy Cooper, Floorcloth Installation, *Abstract Floral with Spiral and Check Border*, 7' x 9' (2 x 2.8 m). Photo by Seth Tice-Lewis

to blend? Have you been looking at other rugs and simply not found one that has the right colors? What color is your floor, and what colors do you want to accent with a rug? Are there any colors in adjacent rooms that you would like to introduce with the floorcloth? Look through some home decor magazines and books to get an idea of what appeals to you. Then scan through the projects in the book for something that goes with your personal decor.

When you find a project that is just right for you, look at the colors that were used. You can make a sketch of the project and substitute your own color choices to see how another version might look. With your color sketch, fabric and wallpaper scraps in hand, you can go directly to the craft-supply store and look at the premixed craft paints.

Look for colors that go with your fabric scraps. You can use a monochromatic theme by staying in the same color but using lighter or darker versions. You can also choose colors that are closely related. If you have blues and blue-greens, try adding yellows or golds. (Remember how you learned to mix primary colors in kindergarten?) If you have a color wheel from painting or quilting, or paint chips from the paint store, you can hold them next to your

materials and get a feel for how other colors might go together. Notice that colors on the opposite side of the color wheel seem to have new life when used next to one another. (Think about red with green or blue with orange).

Purchase the paints you need, along with a few extra choices, if you want to mix your own colors. White and black are both helpful if you plan to do much mixing. One last word on mixing your own colors: make small test batches. This will save you the headache of mixing huge amounts of paint into a color you hate! (It happens all the time so don't feel bad).

What if I want to design my own floorcloth?

Once you've gained some painting confidence, you may want to use your own ideas to create a floorcloth. Floorcloth designs can come from many sources. Look at quilt patterns for both pattern and color. Fabrics, wallpaper, greeting cards, or stationary borders are other good sources for ideas. Clip and save ideas from your favorite home decor or craft magazines, whether it's the motif you like or just the colors. Start a folder for future floorcloths. You may find a border from one source and a center motif from another. It's not uncommon to repeat elements from previous floorcloths, achieving a new look with different colors or with the addition of other design elements.

Kathy Cooper, *Leaves and Scrolls*, 5' x 5' (1.5 m x 1.5 m). Photo by Jerry Anthony

Remember to enjoy the process and let your ideas flow. It's all right to make a change in design or colors in the middle of painting a floorcloth. Sometimes a little painting experience will suggest a new direction in which to take your idea. Let your creative spirit lead you! The most important part of the process is that you find pleasure in your creation. You'll find yourself thinking of all sorts of new ideas for your next project.

So spread out your canvas, paints, and brushes—and get ready to amaze yourself! Yes, you can do this—you can paint a colorful canvas rug to brighten your kitchen, bath, or foyer in a weekend! Why not start this Saturday. Have a great time!

A BRIEF HISTORY OF FLOORCLOTHS

MANY PEOPLE ARE PUZZLED by the word *floorcloth*. Although you won't find the term in the dictionary, floorcloths have been around for more than 200 years. A floorcloth was a common term suggesting a carpet substitute, painted or unpainted. Other common names for a floorcloth are oilcloth, wax cloth, canvas carpet, painted canvas, or painted carpet. A painted floorcloth was made of heavy canvas that had been stretched and sized, then troweled with oil paint, and finished with block printing, stenciling, or hand painting.

The manufacturing of floorcloths was a large and thriving industry in late 18th-century England, regulated by a society of Floor Cloth Manufacturers. The society held monthly meetings to discuss the price of pigments, linseed oil, and canvas, and often cautioned each other about the risk of hiring dishonest workmen.

In America, floorcloths were initially imported from England, which resulted in higher prices and lengthy delivery schedules. Shipping the floorcloths by boat, often during damp, winter weather, could also mean that the merchandise arrived in poor condition. As the market for domestic goods in the new colonies increased, so did the numbers of house painters willing to paint floorcloths in direct competition with the English versions. Newspaper ads frequently appeared offering notice of a new local establishment with skilled painters and the latest floorcloth designs.

Floorcloth patterns were numerous. Many of the early designs were taken from wallpaper patterns, pavement patterns, or woven carpets. They were appreciated for their versatility, function, and ease of care. Floor coverings were not affordable to most people, which made them a treasured household item, often prominently featured in the family portrait. A highly valued floorcloth was frequently listed in household inventories and personal wills, complete with original purchase price. As magazines began to write about and provide instructions on how to make a floorcloth, women began to make their own floorcloths, often stretching the canvas on the side of the barn.

Above: **William Wilkie**, *Nathan Hawley and Family*, Albany, New York, 1801, watercolor on paper, photo by Joseph Levy, collection of the Albany Institute of History and Art; right: **John Carwitham**, *Various Kinds of Floor Decoration*, Plate #8. Photo courtesy of the Library of Congress

GALLERY

"I enjoy making floorcloths because I have limitless artistic freedom, and the finished piece is a very functional, decorative item,"

— Joyce Garlick

Top left: **Fran Rubenstein**, *Just Shapes*, 2½' x 4' (.7 x 1.2 m), photo by Bill Lemke; bottom left: **Francie Riley**, *Palm Leaves*, 2' x 3' (.6 x .9 m), photo by Putnam Imaging; top right: **Joyce Garlick**, *Cups and Saucers*, 1' x 5' (.3 x 1.5 m), photo by Rich-Stele Prolab; bottom right: **Kathy Cooper**, *Abstract Floral Series*, 2½' x 3' (.7 x .9 m), photo by Doyle Bussey

"My designs are primarily about color and how it relates to the adjacent color. My images come from my personal experiences, the garden, my kids, and all of the visual inspiration around me! Color speaks to each of us on a very personal level. Color washes over our senses and takes us somewhere else. I enjoy the response of my viewers when they are inspired by the colors, when they respond to the energy the color gives to them. Color has great power to lift us to a higher level of spirituality."

—Kathy Cooper

"I've been a boat captain for many years, and delivered classic wooden sailboats to all parts. During the off season, I made and sold different crafts, from jewelry to leather bags. As time went on I looked for an art medium that would hold my interest for a long time, one I could take more seriously. I became attached to the canvas sails, and decided there must be a way to use this strong, durable material along with paints to create a functional and useful art object. Floorcloths are the perfect solution."

—*Maggie Vale*

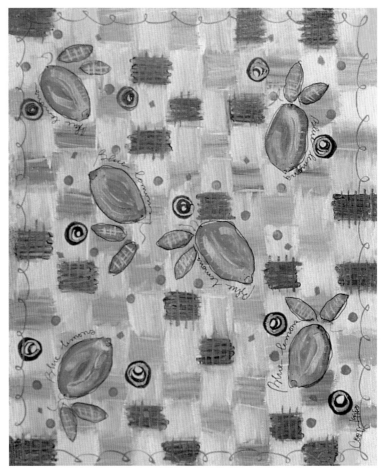

Top left: **Rhonda Kaplan**, *Oak Leaves*, 2' x 4' (.6 x 1.2 m), photo by Jay Friedlander; bottom left: **Francie Riley**, *Sidewalks*, 21" x 34" (53 x 86 cm), photo by Putnam Imaging; top right: **Maggie Vale**, *Geometrix,* 2½' x 3½' (.7 x 1 m), photo by artist; bottom right: **Kathy Cooper**, *Blue Lemons*, 2½' x 3' (.7 x .9 m), photo by Doyle Bussey

"I enjoy painting without the constrictions of space. With floorcloths you have total freedom of a large flat area in which your brush can take off. My inspiration may start with fabrics, photos in gardening magazines, wallpaper, quilts,— even animals"

—*Rhonda Kaplan*

Top left: **Joyce Garlick**, *Random Oaks*, 4' x 6' (1.2 x 1.8 m), photo by Photographic Services; bottom left: **Kathy Cooper**, *Sunflowers and Stripes*, 2½' x 3' (.7 x .9 m), photo by Doyle Bussey; top right: **Fran Rubenstein**, *Hershey Hue*, 3' x 4' (.9 x 1.2 m), photo by Bill Lemke; bottom right: **Rhonda Kaplan**, *Chili Peppers*, 2' x 7' (.6 x 2 m), photo by Jay Friedlander

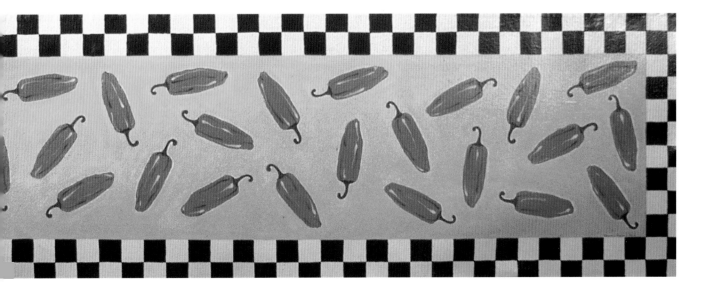

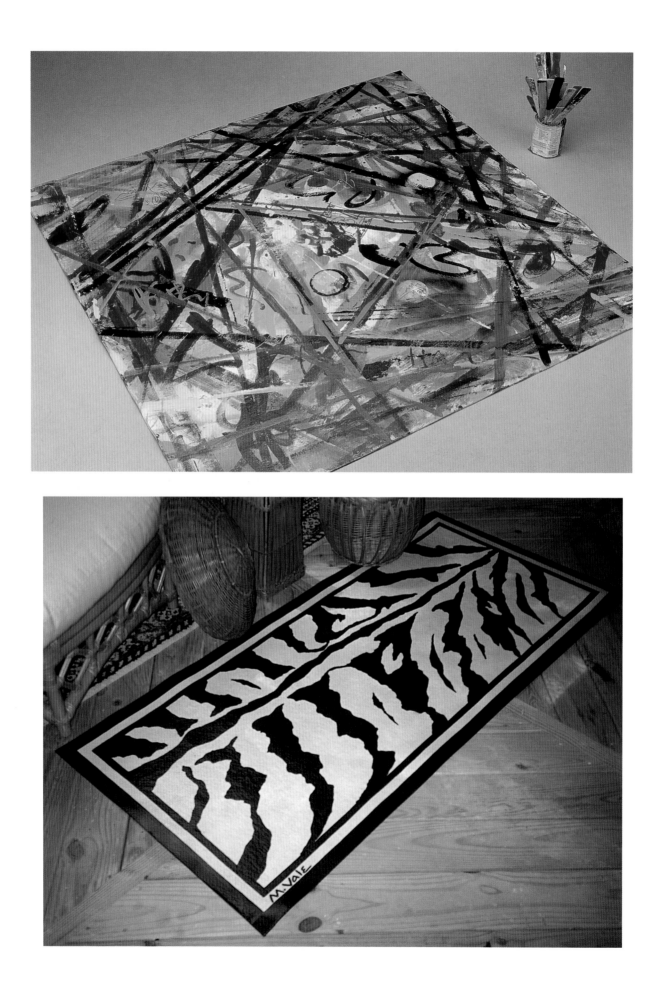

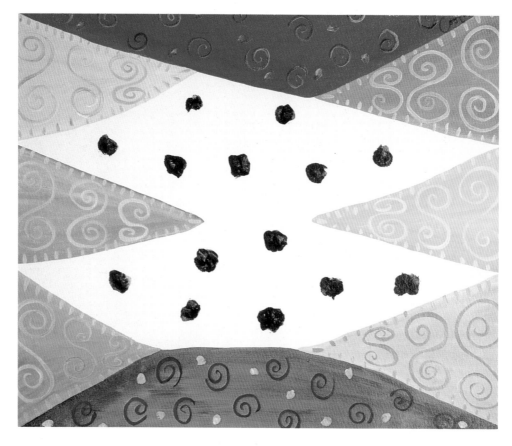

"My inspiration comes from all over. I do thumbnail sketches a lot when I'm riding in a car or sitting on the beach. I switch from painting my daughter's cat in many poses and colors, to wild abstracts, to Matisse influenced designs."

—*Fran Rubenstein*

Top left: **Fran Rubenstein**, *The Real Dropcloth*, 5' x 5' (1.5 x 1.5 m), photo by Bill Lemke; bottom left: **Maggie Vale**, *Zebra,* 3' x 8' (.9 x 2.4 m), photo by artist; top right: **Kathy Cooper**, *Triangles and Dots*, 2½' x 3' (.7 x .9 m), photo by Doyle Bussey; bottom right: **Francie Riley**, *Country Braid*, 21" x 34" (53 x 86 cm), photo by Putnam Imaging

MATERIALS & TOOLS

Clockwise: Assorted rubber and foam stamps, household sponge, white chalk, painter's masking tape, stencils, craft knife, paint pens, star-shaped sponge, artist's bristle brushes, foam brushes, large bristle brush, stencil brush, acrylic craft paints, artist's acrylic paints, foam pouncers, rubber combing tool, bristle brush, acrylic varnish, paint tray, paste wax and soft rag, matte medium, soft cloth

All about Canvas
PREPRIMED

For each project included in this book you'll find a materials list. To make any of these floorcloths, you'll need canvas. The quickest, easiest way to make a floorcloth in a weekend is to buy *preprimed canvas*, available at art- or craft-supply stores, and through mail-order catalogs. Preprimed canvas is available in several weights; the heavier weight canvas is the right choice for a floorcloth, and the thinner canvas is suitable for place mats and table runners. Having tried several kinds, I recommend using Dixie 123 for a floorcloth (see the supplier list on page 79), a

sturdy 12-ounce cotton duck with substantial texture, double primed on one side. Purchase enough canvas for your floorcloth, using the desired finished measurements, plus 4 inches (10 cm) extra in length and width for the hem.

Preprimed canvas also comes in two varieties—*primed on one side* and *primed on two sides*. The primed side (s) looks white (that's the painted ground on which you will paint). Primed on one side has a natural side (that's the side that goes on the floor). Primed on two sides looks white on both sides, but one side is smoother and less textured (that's the side on which you will paint). Primed on two sides canvas is referred to as *floorcloth canvas*. It has a stiffer feel, and may seem less flexible on the floor—more like a piece of linoleum.

Preprimed canvas is prepared under tension. It has been stretched and primed, then heat set in large ovens. Canvas primed on one side is susceptible to water damage if the untreated side sits on puddles of water. Most of the time this is not a problem; but if you live with elephants that tend to dribble buckets of water every day, you should probably choose canvas primed on both sides.

UNPRIMED

You can also purchase *unprimed canvas* yardage at art-supply stores. Unprimed canvas is also listed by a number that corresponds to the weight of the fabric. (Usually the lower number is a heavier weight, but it's best to compare actual samples.) Most floorcloth artists use a #10 or a #12, which are both readily available. If you use unprimed canvas, you will probably want to prime it before you paint your design; priming gives the canvas a smoother surface on which to paint. You don't need to stretch the canvas when you prime it, provided the primer you use isn't too thin

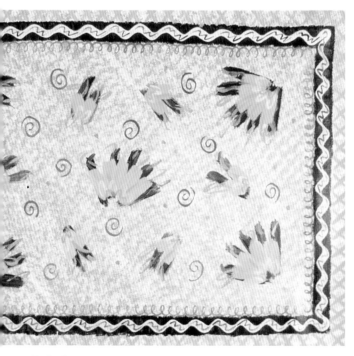

Kathy Cooper, *Abstract Floral with Ribbon Border*, 5' x 7' (1.5 x 2 m).
Photo by Doyle Bussey

(watery) and is not oil based (oil-based paint products require a different process to seal and protect the canvas from the oil paints).

PRIMERS

Most artists use a prepared primer called *acrylic gesso* which is made of acrylic polymer, calcium carbonate, and titanium dioxide (for white). Acrylic gesso also comes in other colors. Depending on the brand, it's either ready to apply or ready to dilute with water. It should be about the consistency of thinned sour cream. Apply the primer with a house paint roller or a paintbrush. (For more information about priming, please refer to *The Complete Book of Floorcloths*, Lark Books, 1997).

All about Creating a Hem

Preprimed canvas is easiest to use because you can jump right in and make a floorcloth with very little preparation. Most of the projects in this book start with a prepared canvas hemmed to size before the design is applied.

You can make a floorcloth with and without a hem. Floorcloth canvas (primed on both sides) is fairly stiff, and can be left unhemmed. However, over time you will probably notice that the corners will start to curl when they are kicked up, which might cause you to trip. Hemming the floorcloth encourages the floorcloth to lay flat, and results in a more attractive and functional area rug.

To hem your canvas you will need a yardstick to measure with, a right angle to create clean corners, a pencil, a pair of sharp scissors, and double-stick carpet tape. Double-stick tape is used to lay carpet, and is available at most home improvement and hardware stores. The tape comes in different widths; you'll want to match your hem width to the width of the tape since it's hard to cut this very sticky tape into thinner widths. Most of the projects in this book use a 2-inch (5 cm) hem, which means you'll want to purchase 2-inch-wide (5 cm) tape.

Double-stick carpet tape makes a nice, clean hem, and allows you to do the job in minutes. Glued hems often buckle, especially on untreated canvas. For best results, follow the detailed instructions about hemming a floorcloth starting on page 22.

All about Paints

You can paint a floorcloth with many types of paint. Those listed here are readily available and easy to use.

CRAFT PAINTS

Craft paints are an excellent and easy choice, and come in a wide variety of colors. You'll find a large selection of premixed acrylic craft paints at craft-supply stores. These work wonderfully for your design painting, are suitable for many painting techniques, and don't require any special treatment. You can use them right out of the bottle. They come in many premixed colors (or can be mixed to make new colors), and they clean up with water.

ARTIST'S ACRYLIC PAINTS

If you prefer, you may use artist's acrylic paints. These come either in jars as a liquid or in tubes as a paste. There will be many colors to choose from, too, though probably not as many as the premixed craft paints. Tube paints will require some *medium* as a thinner—either a matte or gloss medium; these can be helpful if the liquid paint is too thick. You need to add enough medium so that the tube paint will have a consistency with which you can paint. You can thin paints with water only slightly or they will become too watery and messy for many of the techniques used in these projects. Don't use watercolors or other paints that may bleed when you varnish the floorcloth (these paints are resoluable when dry). If you already have some paints on hand, be sure to test them for suitability with your varnish before using them to paint your floorcloth.

LATEX HOUSEPAINTS

Latex housepaint is a good choice if you're painting a background color on a large floorcloth, or need even coverage. Latex housepaint also works well if you want your floorcloth to have a glossier surface. You can use interior paint if you already have some. Exterior latex is more flexible, an important characteristic if you'll be rolling and unrolling your floorcloths.

PAINT FINISHES

Select a paint finish that is suitable for the type of painting you'll be doing. Flat finish paint works fine for basic painting. But if, for example, you're trying to create a faux finish effect, and you need the design paint to slide around and have more working time before it dries, choose a paint with a low-gloss finish so that the faux paint won't soak into the surface too quickly. Test high-sheen paints to make sure they're compatible with the acrylic varnish you'll be applying to the finished floorcloth (see page 26). Sometimes very deep colors and very glossy paints don't take the acrylic varnish well.

MIXING COLORS

If you have a color wheel it will help you determine which paints to mix to achieve a certain color. In general you may want to purchase the primary colors (red, yellow, blue) and maybe some secondary colors (green, purple, orange), along with black and white. Each project in this book features a color template; to match the project colors exactly, you can simply take the book to the store, and find matching paint colors or colors you can mix to achieve a match with the project colors.

MATTE MEDIUMS AND PAINT CONDITIONERS

Matte medium is a clear polymer that is used to thin acrylic paints. It also works well for sealing masking tape, whenever you're trying to create a crisp line (see page 29 for details). Matte mediums can be applied with regular paintbrushes, dry clear, and clean up easily with water.

Another paint product that can be helpful is *paint conditioner*, or *glazing liquid*, available at paint stores. It's similar to matte medium but is more liquid, and is used to prolong the drying time of paint. You can use it to thin acrylic paint, or add it to paint to create a thin colored glaze that you might use for faux painting.

All about Painting Tools

You can paint a floorcloth without any special tools, using items you may already have in your house, such as foam brushes or household sponges. Just for fun you can try a few special new tools as needed, depending on the project or design.

You'll find all kinds of paintbrushes, stencils, stamps, pouncers, markers, and other painting tools at your local art- or craft-supply store. Familiarize yourself with the store's selection of stencil brushes, fine detail brushes, sponge brushes, foam brushes, textured faux painting tools, rubber combs, sponge stamps, foam stamps, rubber stamps, precut stencils, masking tape, and other painting supplies. Many of the easy-to-use stamp or stencil kits can produce lovely designs on a floorcloth with a minimal amount of painting skill. You can also draw on floorcloths with permanent markers and paint pens; make sure they're not water soluble, or the varnish coating on the floorcloth will cause the markers to bleed.

The supplier list on page 79 includes mail-order catalogs that carry wide selections of painting supplies. For more information about painting materials and techniques, see pages 28 to 31.

All about Varnish

There are many choices for *acrylic varnish* sold at art- and craft-supply stores. Most premixed craft paints are designed to be used with certain acrylic polymer finishes. These varnishes are sold under a variety of

Left: **Kathy Cooper**, *Journal Drawings with Filigree Border*, 5' x 6' (1.5 x 1.8 m); above: **Kathy Cooper**, *Night Sky Series*, 1½' x 3'(.4 x .9 m). Both Photos by Doyle Bussey

names, such as acrylic varnish, acrylic clear finish, or acrylic polyurethane. You can also look for acrylic varnishes in the section of the store that features artist's acrylic paints. All of these acrylic varnishes will likely cost more than the quart containers of varnish designed for wood surfaces that are sold at paint stores, but they will be much more flexible and will help your floorcloth to last longer without cracking.

Most acrylic polymer varnishes look milky when wet, and dry clear. You can apply them right out of the container or pour some into a plastic bowl or foam tray. Apply the varnish with a clean paintbrush. A flat synthetic bristle brush works well; stay away from foam brushes for this application because they tend to disintegrate with use. Refer to page 26 for complete details.

All about Paste Wax

After you apply an acrylic varnish to the painted floorcloth, and it has thoroughly dried, you need to finish with a good-quality, clear paste wax, available at hardware stores. Paste wax provides two important qualities to the floorcloth: it makes the acrylic varnish harder by sealing the varnish from the air, and it helps to keep the floorcloth cleaner. Once you have applied a coat of paste wax, you can safely scrub the surface of the floorcloth to clean the dirt, and you can rewax as needed. Ask for *bowling alley wax* which is a white color; it can be used with light colors without discoloring the painted finish. You will need clean rags to apply the wax to the floorcloth and to buff it. See page 26 for more information.

Anything Else?

With materials in hand and a place in your house where you can spread out, you'll also need newspaper or plastic sheeting to cover the floor or table, a water bucket, and some paint rags or paper towels. Put on your favorite music, take the phone off the hook, and get ready to have fun!

FLOORCLOTH BASICS

TO MAKE ANY FLOORCLOTH in this book, or one that you design yourself, you'll need to purchase enough preprimed canvas for the desired size plus an appropriate hem allowance on all sides of the floorcloth. As mentioned earlier, the hem allowance for these rugs is 2 inches (5 cm) on each side. This hem will match the 2-inch-wide (5 cm) carpet tape that you'll use to create the hem.

STEP 1: MEASURING AND MARKING THE HEM

YOU WILL NEED

Preprimed canvas

Pencil

Straightedge or yardstick

Right angle

Sharp scissors

Your preprimed canvas should be the size of your desired finished floorcloth, plus a 2-inch (5 cm) hem on all four sides. (This accounts for the extra 4 inches [10 cm] on the length and width of the canvas you purchased.)

1 Lay the preprimed canvas, painted side up, on a smooth, clean surface. Measure 2 inches (5 cm) in from the edge—this will create a 2-inch-wide (5 cm) hem—and lay a straightedge along these marks (side 1). Pencil a line along the side of the straight edge, letting your line extend into the hem allowance on sides 2 and 4.

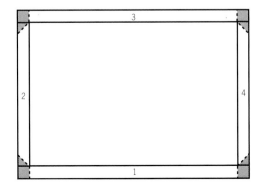

corner you should have two lines that intersect each other. If any of your corners do not appear square, or if your measurements do not match, now is the time to adjust them. Simply pick the straightest side, remeasure, and recheck the corners to make sure they are at right angles.

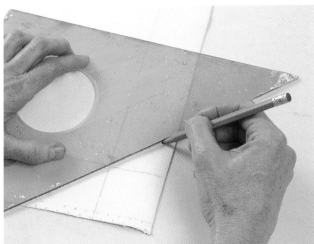

2 On the left end of this line, measure 2 inches (5 cm) in from the outside edge and make a mark. Take the right angle and set it on the mark with a 2-inch (5 cm) hem allowance along the outside edge. Lay the straightedge over the right angle to create a perpendicular line (side 2). Pencil this line along the side of the straightedge, letting your line extend into the hem allowance for side 3.

3 Measure the length of side 1, starting at the left-hand corner on side 2, and mark your desired length. Make a small pencil mark on the right hand corner, allowing for a 2-inch (5 cm) hem on that perpendicular edge, as well. Set the right angle on the pencil mark, with the 2-inch (5 cm) hem allowance on the outside of the corner. Lay the straightedge on top of the right angle, and pencil a line along this edge (side 4). Let your line extend into the hem allowance for side 3.

4 Measure the length for the short side of your floorcloth along side 2. Make a small mark; then, alongside 4, make another mark. Allow a 2-inch (5 cm) hem on the outside edge of these marks.

5 Lay the right angle on the top left-hand corner mark on side 2. Lay the straightedge on top of the right angle, connecting it to the other mark on the top right-hand side on side 4. Pencil a line along the straightedge, connecting these marks (side 3). Let your line extend into the hem allowance on sides 2 and 4.

6 Your canvas should now have a penciled shape that is either square or rectangular, with a 2-inch (5 cm) border showing all the way around. On each

7 After you've checked your measurements, go back to each corner with a right angle and pencil. Lay the right angle across each intersection and mark a line, only on the short hem. When trimmed, this will create something like an envelope flap on the short ends.

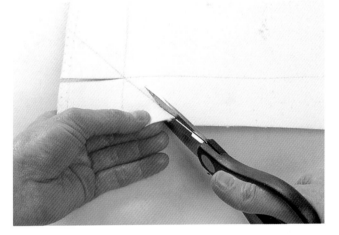

8 Trim along the line of the flap and along the corner. Your hem should have two long sides with a straight 2-inch (5 cm) border that ends flush on the corner. There should be two shorter sides (if it's a rectangle shape) that have an angled 2-inch (5 cm) hem that looks like a wide envelope flap.

STEP 2: HEMMING THE FLOORCLOTH

YOU WILL NEED

Canvas marked with a hem line

Straightedge or yardstick

Double-stick carpet tape

Sharp scissors

1 Lay the straightedge on the canvas along the pencil line that creates the hem. Fold the canvas over the straightedge to crease the hem. When you have done this on all four sides, flip the canvas to the underside, primed side down, and pre-crease it in the opposite direction, again using the straightedge. You should have a folded edge along your pencil line that makes the hem easy to see.

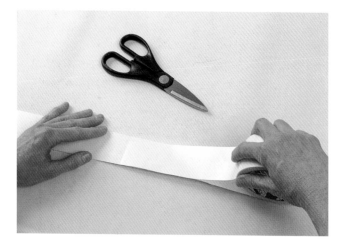

2 Lay a strip of carpet tape along the inside (the unprimed side) of one of the long hem lines. Trim

any excess tape off the end. Peel back the protective coating on the tape.

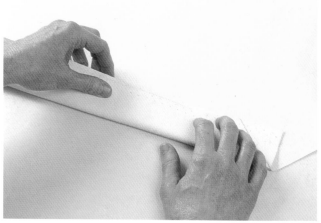

3 Fold the long hem to the underside of the canvas. Use your hand or the roll of tape to rub up and down along the hem to remove any air bubbles. Voila! You now have a hem! Repeat this process on the other long hem.

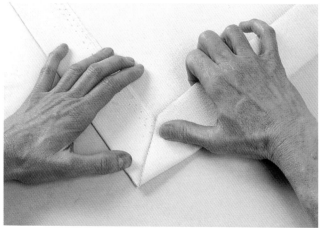

4 Run the tape along one of the angled ends. Trim the excess tape off the angled end. Fold this hem the way you did in steps 1 and 2; let the hem overlap the two long sides on each corner. You should have nice crisp corners. Repeat this process on the other angled end.

STEP 3: PREPARING A BACKGROUND COLOR

YOU WILL NEED

Hemmed floorcloth

Craft paint or latex paint

Foam or bristle paintbrush

Newspaper or plastic sheeting

1 Some of the floorcloth projects in this book begin by painting a colored background on the hemmed floorcloth. If you select one of these projects, lay your hemmed floorcloth on a protected painting surface, which you have covered with newspaper or plastic sheeting. Apply a thin, even coat of the desired background color. Take care not to let the paint puddle over the edge or it will stick to the newspaper. Let dry.

2 If necessary, apply a second coat to achieve a more even coverage.

STEP 4: DRAWING YOUR DESIGN

YOU WILL NEED

Prepared and hemmed floorcloth

2B pencil or white chalk

Art gum eraser

Straightedge or yardstick

Templates or copies (optional)

Carbon paper (optional)

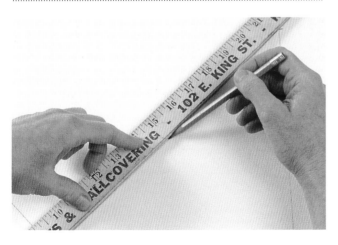

1 Some of the projects in this book include directions for marking the complete design onto the floorcloth, while others are designs that do not require advance marking. You can use a 2B pencil or white chalk to mark as needed. Pencil lightly, so that mistakes can be erased with an art gum eraser; wipe off the white chalk with a damp sponge. The need to sketch the design first will vary with the type of design and the intended look of the completed floorcloth.

2 For projects using templates, you can enlarge the design template on a copier. Use carbon paper under the copy and lightly go over the design with a pencil, as shown on page 59.

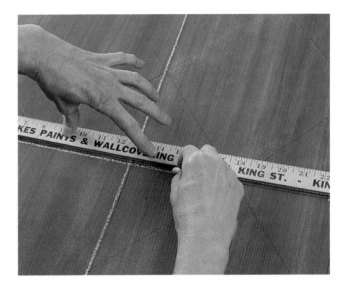

3 Sometimes you will need to establish a center point on the floorcloth. To do this, make a measurement on each side that represents the center point of that side, and mark the points with a pencil or chalk. Lay a straightedge across the center point to the opposite side, and make a small line in the center of the floorcloth on that line. Repeat in the opposite direction—you should now have a small cross in the center of the floorcloth representing the center point. You can measure off this point in any direction as needed.

4 If you are measuring from the outside edge of your floorcloth, you can use your hem as the point from which you mark a border, checks, or other patterns. That is why it's important to get a good, even hem.

STEP 5: PAINTING THE DESIGN

YOU WILL NEED

Hemmed floorcloth, marked as needed

Painting supplies and tools, as specified in each project

Paint

Paint trays

Rags

1 Now comes the really fun part! Your design can be chosen from one of the projects in this book or from your imagination. If you choose, you can work from a thumbnail sketch or an elaborate full-scale color sample. You can paint fast and furiously with big quick strokes or slow and meticulously with delicate strokes. The choice is totally up to you.

2 In general it's a good idea to think of the background color as setting the stage; each layer of pattern you add to the background becomes part of the scenery, and then the details are added last. One of the great freedoms in painting a floorcloth is that if you aren't happy with your results, you can paint over it! Keep some scraps of canvas on hand to experiment on, and then jump in with your ideas.

STEP 6: VARNISHING YOUR FLOORCLOTH

YOU WILL NEED

Finished, dry, painted floorcloth

Clean sponge

Acrylic varnish

Paint tray or plastic bowl (optional)

Clean, flat synthetic bristle paintbrush

Hairdryer (optional)

After all of your design work is complete and you have let the floorcloth dry, it's time to apply a few coats of varnish to protect your painting. Look for an acrylic varnish that is used with acrylic paints, preferably not too glossy.

1 Make sure your paint has had time to completely dry. Sometimes the paint will feel dry to the touch, but is not yet cured. Wipe the floorcloth with a clean, damp sponge to remove any dirt.

2 Apply some varnish to a very small area of the floorcloth to make sure the paint won't run. Then apply a thin coat of acrylic varnish with a clean, flat bristle brush, following the manufacturer's recommendations. In general, acrylic varnish needs to be applied with a gentle touch in thin, even coats. Don't be alarmed if the wet varnish appears milky; it will dry clear. Begin on one side of the floorcloth and brush slowly in long strokes, taking great care not to leave large puddles of varnish. Over-brushing acrylic varnish will trap air bubbles and cause the finish to appear cloudy when dry. Puddles may also dry cloudy. Note: The number of coats of varnish you'll need will depend on the brand you use. Make sure the surface feels smooth to the touch so that it will be easy to clean.

3 Set the floorcloth aside to dry, or use a hairdryer to speed the drying process. Drying time will vary according to the weather. Give each coat of varnish enough time to harden, even if you do speed the drying time with a hairdryer.

STEP 7: APPLYING PASTE WAX TO YOUR FLOORCLOTH

YOU WILL NEED

Dry, varnished floorcloth

Clear, bowling alley paste wax

Clean rags

Acrylic varnish benefits from a coat of clear, bowling alley paste wax. The wax will protect the varnish and make it easier to keep the floorcloth clean. Bowling alley paste wax has no color, and won't discolor the painted surface.

1 After the varnished floorcloth is completely dry, apply a thin coat of clear paste wax with a small, dry rag.

2 Let the floorcloth air dry; then buff to a sheen with a clean, dry rag.

STEP 8: INSTALLING AND USING YOUR FLOORCLOTH

When you have finished making your floorcloth, you're ready to enjoy it. Before you put it in its intended location, take the time to follow these brief instructions.

YOU WILL NEED

Vacuum cleaner

Damp mop

Thin rubber pad, or rug gripper tape the size of the floorcloth

Double-stick carpet tape

Mild soap or cleanser

Old-fashioned scrub brush (optional)

1 Clean the floor where you'll be placing the floor-cloth. Vacuum and damp mop if necessary. A small piece of grit can cause a bump to appear on the painted surface of the floorcloth. If, after you've installed the floorcloth, you see a bump, check the back of the floorcloth or the floor, and remove the grit.

2 Place the rubber pad on the floor; this will prevent the floorcloth from slipping, and give a little extra cushioning under your feet. You can use a thin weblike pad designed to go under carpets; simply trim it to the correct size. If you want, you can use double-stick carpet tape to adhere the rubber pad to the back of the floorcloth. Another choice is rug gripper tape, which is sticky and meshlike. You run it in strips along the back sides of the hem.

3 Place the floorcloth on the floor and enjoy!

4 When you clean the room, sweep over the floor-cloth. If you use an upright vacuum on the rest of the room, be careful not to catch the corners of the floorcloth. You can also use a damp mop or a sponge to clean the floorcloth. Use a mild soap, if necessary. If you need to scrub the canvas, use a gentle touch and an old-fashioned scrub brush. Take care not to let the water puddle under the floorcloth. Use commercial cleaners with care; they shouldn't be too gritty, or you can damage the paint. Read the product label carefully to make sure these cleaners are compatible with acrylic finishes. Rewax the floorcloth as needed.

MAKING THE PROJECTS IN THIS BOOK

Each project features a complete list of the materials, supplies, and tools you will need. For all the floorcloths, you will begin with a hemmed canvas of a certain size: this topic is covered on pages 22 to 24. You are welcome to make any of the rugs larger or smaller, but you will need to adjust the measurements in the instructions accordingly. For the table runner and place mats, you start with unhemmed canvas. The written instructions and step-by-step photographs guide you through the process of painting that project. If special techniques are used, you will be referred to the specific pages that describe that topic. You will finish all the projects the same way—by varnishing and waxing them. Refer to pages 26 and 27 for details. It is always a good idea to read through the project instructions one or two times before you begin; that way you will have a mental map of where you are going.

PAINTING TECHNIQUES

EVEN IF YOU HAVEN'T painted anything for a long time (or ever!), you can paint fabulous-looking floorcloths. The projects in this book require only a few simple painting skills which are described in this section. Some of the methods may be more familiar to you than others. All of them are easy, and will help you create a beautiful floorcloth in a weekend.

Transferring Your Design

You can use several techniques to transfer your design to the prepared canvas.

CARBON PAPER OUTLINE

If you're trying to copy and trace an image or pattern, first enlarge it on a copier to the size indicated.

Position the copy over a piece of carbon paper in the correct area on your floorcloth; then lightly trace over the lines with a pencil. When you're finished, you'll have something to follow that resembles an outlined paint-by-number image.

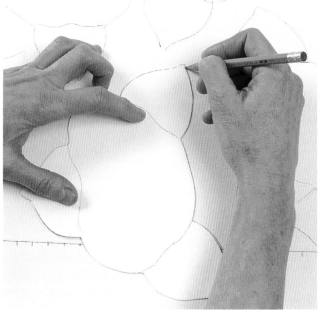

PAPER OR CANVAS TEMPLATE

You can transfer a design, too, by creating a paper or canvas template. First enlarge the drawing on a copier to the size indicated. Now cut out the design. Or you can place the cutout design on a piece of scrap canvas, outline around the template, and cut a second template out of canvas, which is much studier. Position the template on the floorcloth and trace around it with pencil or white chalk.

You can also use a straightedge to measure out your design, if necessary. This works well for checks, diagonals, or borders. You can make light marks on the canvas with a 2B pencil or white chalk. Use an art gum eraser to eliminate unwanted pencil lines and a damp sponge to wipe off chalk marks.

FINDING THE CENTER POINT

You may need to establish the center point on your floorcloth before measuring a design. For information on finding the center point, see page 25.

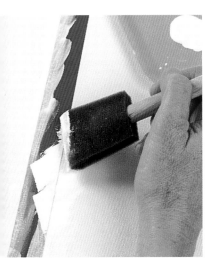

Blocking Out with Masking Tape

Masking tape is a great tool for many paint techniques. To mask out a straight line, use *low-tack painter's masking tape* (usually comes in blue) and run a line on your floorcloth; this tape won't leave any gummy residue when you remove it later. Seal the taped line with either the background paint or clear matte medium. This will keep the design color from seeping under your tape line. When the sealer is dry, paint your straight line in the desired color, up to and on top of the tape. Let dry and peel off the tape to reveal a crisp, clean line.

Masking tape is also valuable for holding a stencil in place or creating a masked shape, such as a large check. For best results, seal the tape before painting the masked shapes.

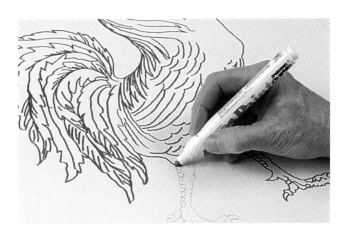

with a light touch; paint pens can clog up, and if you press too firmly on a clogged pen, you'll wind up with a puddle of paint!

There are many brands of paint pens and markers; choose one that is waterproof. There are a number of brands of opaque paint pens available that come in a variety of bright colors. Black permanent laundry markers work well, too.

Test your pen or marker on a scrap of canvas, then apply a coat of acrylic varnish. If the pen is not waterproof, it will bleed under the varnish. Make sure the design paint on the floorcloth is dry before you try to draw on top of it.

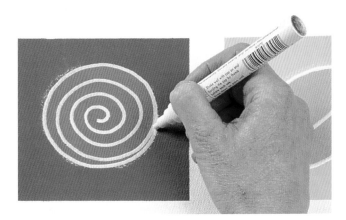

Paint Pens for Drawing

You can use paint pens to create many special effects on your floorcloths. Paint pens and permanent markers are also a great way to personalize your floorcloth by writing your name, favorite sayings, or a special poem that inspires you. They are also handy for creating details, such as the ones on the Twin Roosters floorcloth (page 42) and are much easier to use than a paintbrush! Hold the pen firmly, but use it

Hand Painting

Select a paintbrush for hand painting that matches the effect you want to achieve—a wide foam or bristle brush for large strokes or a fine-point artist's bristle brush for small strokes. Artist's brushes come in many shapes and sizes. Select what you feel comfortable painting with. If you feel awkward using an artist's brush, try a foam brush. Foam brushes are user friendly and work great for painting checks and stripes. A foam pouncer (looks like a stencil brush with a sponge on the end) makes it easy to paint little circles or grapes!

Paint Blending

Many of these projects use simple paint blending techniques that create very painterly effects.

WET-ON-WET BLENDING

Wet-on-wet blending is a process in which two wet colors of paint are allowed to touch and slightly mix on the canvas to create a new color. Use a clean foam or bristle brush for each color. The important thing to remember in wet blending is to use colors that will work well together so that you don't end up with a muddy mess! Stick with colors that are in the same family, such as the gold and beige used in the leopard floorcloth (see page 54), or with one color that is related by the two colors on either side of it, such as orange with red and yellow. Brush the second color up to and adjacent to the first color, and then let your brush slightly mix both colors.

DRY-BRUSH MIXING

Another popular paint mixing technique is *dry brush mixing*. Similar to the wet-on-wet blending method, the colors are allowed to blend on the canvas while you're painting; the only difference in dry brush mixing is that the colors are also allowed to mix on the brush. To do this, dip a clean foam or bristle brush in one color on one side of the brush, and dip it again into another color on the other side of the brush. Then start painting. This technique creates a wonderful textured finish and works especially well with acrylic tube paints. Work your color and let it blend as you paint. Your brush will need more paint as you go along, so try to keep the colors on the same side of the brush each time. (See the finished Sunflowers and Swirls floorcloth, page 44.)

Stenciling

Many of the projects in this book utilize stencils. You can cut your own out of *clear plastic stencil film*, sold in art- and craft-supply stores. Select a thickness that won't tear easily but can be cut with scissors or a matte knife. Cuticle scissors work great for cutting stencils. There are many attractive and interesting precut stencils available as well.

To print with your stencil, use a *spray stencil adhesive* or masking tape to hold the stencil firmly in place on the floorcloth. You can use a stencil brush, sponge, or foam pouncer to apply the paint. Apply the paint lightly inside the stencil, letting your application cover the clear plastic film as well.

Stamping

Several of the floorcloth projects use commercial stamps or handmade stamps from potatoes, sponges, and packing foam. These are all easy to use to create dramatic effects. Use a small sponge or brush to load the stamp with paint. Test your print on a scrap of canvas to get the right paint application. With a firm hand, gently press straight down in the desired location. Carefully lift the stamp straight up so that the painted image doesn't smear. When you have made a few practice runs and feel confident, proceed to stamp directly onto your floorcloth.

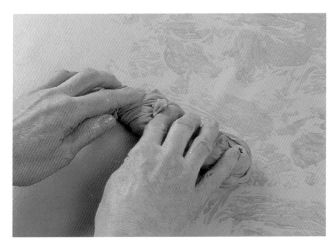

Rag Rolling

Many faux-paint techniques, such as *rag rolling*, use an ordinary household item, in this case a soft, rolled, rag, to add additional texture to the paint. First dampen the rag, then dip it into a colored glaze (see page 66 for a glaze recipe). Twist the rag and wring it out. Using a motion similar to a paint roller, roll the painted rag over the background color. Keep the rag twisted, with the ends tucked in. Periodically, dip the rag in the glaze

color again to achieve consistent coverage. See page 66 for the finished floorcloth done this way. Rag rolling is a simple technique that can be effective in softening the look of a solid background color.

Combing

Like rag rolling, *combing* uses a colored glaze or paint on top of a base color, along with a simple rubber combing tool to achieve a textured effect. Thin the top color with paint conditioner, then brush it over the dry base color. While the paint is still wet, drag the comb through the top color to create a striped effect. You can vary the direction of the comb and add additional texture. The completed floorcloth appears on page 48.

Spatter Paint

It's all in the wrist! The best way to spatter paint is to load your brush with wet paint and gently tap in the direction you wish to splatter. Sometimes you'll need to thin the paint with a little paint conditioner to get good splatters and not globs! Be sure to rotate yourself around the floorcloth so the spatters aren't all in one direction. This method is fun, but watch out for the rest of your room—splatters travel far!

Stenciled Leaves

DESIGN: **JOYCE GARLICK**

*Motifs from nature complement any decor. This stunning
floorcloth, painted with bright colors and simple stencils, will help
you bring the outdoors inside in a most appealing way.*

YOU WILL NEED

Hemmed floorcloth, 36 x 48 inches (90 x 120 cm)	Yardstick	Scissors
	White chalk	Craft knife
Paints: White and red	Painter's masking tape	Stencil brush or stiff-bristle paintbrush
Foam or bristle paintbrush	Pencil	Varnish
Paint trays	Clear plastic stencil film	Paste wax

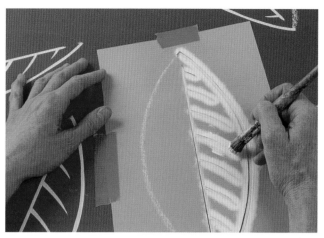

1 Paint the hemmed floorcloth red, and let dry. Measure a 1-inch-wide (2.5 cm) border that is 2 inches (5 cm) from the hemmed edge. Pencil in the border, and tape around the lines with masking tape. Seal with matte medium, and let dry. Paint the border white, and let dry. Remove the tape.

3 Trace the leaf template onto stencil film, and pencil in leaf veins on half the stencil. Cut out the stencil. Tape it over one of the leaf shapes on the floorcloth. Use the stencil brush to apply white paint over the cut half of the stencil, and let dry. Remove the tape. Place the stencil over another leaf shape, tape it down, and brush on the paint. Continue in this way until you have painted the stencil pattern on all the leaf shapes. Rinse the paint off the stencil and dry it thoroughly.

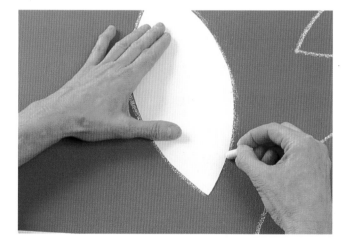

2 Enlarge the leaf template (page 74) to the size indicated, and cut it out. Outline the leaf shape randomly in the center field with chalk. TIP: For a sturdier template, outline the cutout leaf on a scrap of canvas, cut out the shape, and use this as your leaf template.

4 Flip the stencil over and tape it over a leaf shape. Brush paint over the stencil to paint the other half of the leaf. Continue in this way until you have stenciled in the other half of all the leaf shapes. Let dry. Varnish and wax your floorcloth.

Flower and Leaf Checkerboard

DESIGNER: **JOANNA BRITT**

This delightful pattern uses a checkerboard with flowers and leaves alternated on bright squares of color. The trick here is that flowers can be suggested with a simple swirl of a paint pen over a painted circle.

YOU WILL NEED

Hemmed floorcloth, 24 x 36 inches (60 x 90 cm)	Paints: Purple, orange, green, pink, and white	Scissors
Yardstick		White chalk
Pencil	Paint trays	White paint pen
Painter's masking tape	Cup, can, or plastic lid, 3½ inches (9 cm) in diameter	Varnish
Foam or bristle paintbrushes		Paste wax

1 On the hemmed floorcloth measure every 6 inches (15 cm) both vertically and horizontally. Using these marks as the center point, make a grid with painter's masking tape. Run the tape around the outer edge to create the border. Seal with white paint, and let dry. Then paint the alternate squares purple, and let dry. Paint the other squares orange, and let dry. Remove the tape.

3 Enlarge the leaf on page 74, and create a leaf template on paper or canvas. Outline the shape with chalk on all the orange squares. Note the way the leaf shape is alternated. Paint the leaves green, and let dry.

2 On the purple squares, trace around the round object with chalk. Paint the circles pink, and let dry.

4 Outline the leaf shapes with the white paint pen and draw a center line on each leaf. Outline the rose shapes with white paint pen and continue the line to create a white spiral on each rose. Let dry. Varnish and wax your floorcloth.

Bee and Diamond Runner

DESIGNERS: **MICEY MOYER AND POLLY EAGAN**

The diamond pattern, stamped bees, and rich tones of red and gold add up to one gorgeous rug! Although elegant to look at, this floor runner is incredibly easy to paint.

YOU WILL NEED

Hemmed floorcloth, 29 x 77 inches (73 x 195 cm)

Foam or bristle paintbrush

Fine-pointed artist's paintbrush

Paints: Red and gold

Paint trays

Yardstick

Black marker or white chalk

Gold paint pen (optional)

Bee rubber stamp

Small round pouncer or stencil brush

Painter's masking tape (optional)

Varnish

Paste wax

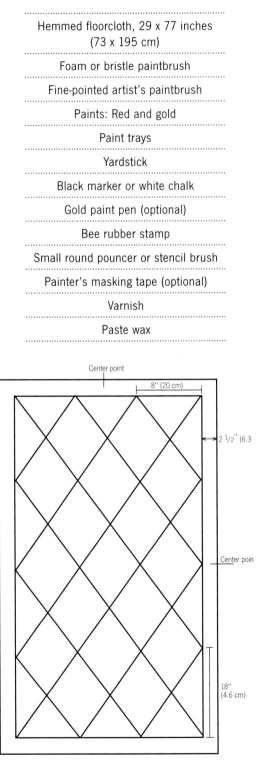

Center point

8" (20 cm)

2 1/2" (6.3

Center poin

18" (4.6 cm)

1 Paint the hemmed runner red, and let dry. Mark a 2½-inch (6.3 cm) border all around the

floorcloth. Measure for the diamonds by marking a center point on the interior field of the long sides of the floorcloth, using black marker or white chalk. On each side of the center, mark another point at 18 inches (46 cm). This should give you four spaces, each 18 inches (46 cm) long. Now measure the center point of the interior field on the short sides and mark. Then measure 4 inches (10 cm) off the center in each direction. This should create three spaces, each 8 inches (20 cm) long. Use a yardstick to connect the points diagonally, beginning with the corner mark on one long side connecting with the first mark in from the corner on the opposite diagonal, as shown in the drawing.

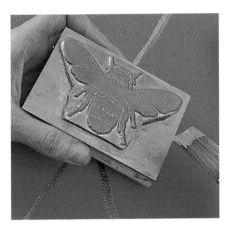

4 Brush gold paint onto the bee rubber stamp.

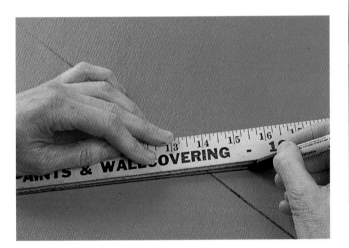

2 Continue drawing lines until you have diamonds all over your runner.

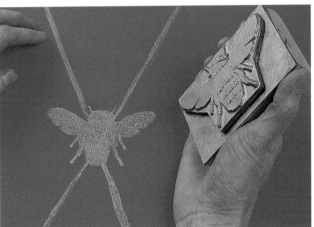

5 Randomly stamp a few of the diamond intersections with the bee stamp. On a few of the other intersections, stamp a circle in gold paint using either a stencil brush or small pouncer. Let dry.

3 Paint the lines with gold paint and a thin brush. If your hand is unsteady, you could also use a paint pen. Let dry.

6 Paint the border gold, and let dry. If your hand is unsteady, you can tape off the border before you paint it. Varnish and wax your floorcloth.

Yellow Roses and Stripes Floorcloth

DESIGNER: **RHONDA KAPLAN**

Yellow roses have a way of adding cheer and charm to any room. Using a template, some basic painting skills, and a steady hand for the stripes, you can have roses everyday of your life, thanks to this beautiful rug.

YOU WILL NEED

Hemmed floorcloth, 24 x 30 inches (60 x 75 cm)	Scissors	Small foam paintbrush
Yardstick	Paints: Light and dark yellow, light and dark green, white, and black	Small artist's paintbrush
Pencil	Paint trays	Varnish
		Paste wax

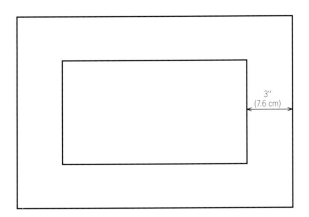

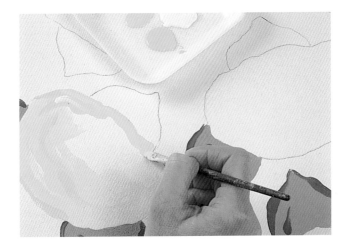

1 Pencil a 3-inch-wide (7.5 cm) border all around the hemmed floorcloth, and then mark off stripes ½ inch (1.3 cm) wide.

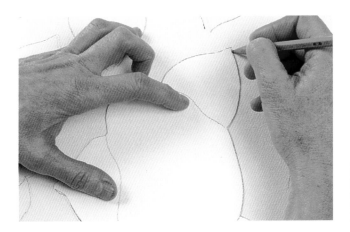

2 Enlarge the flower (page 74) to the size indicated, and cut it out. Outline the flower all over the floorcloth, using the finished rug as a guide for placement.

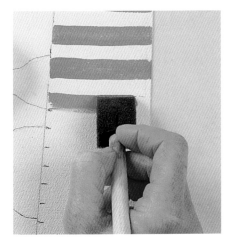

3 Use the foam brush to paint the stripes light green, and let dry.

4 Use the small bristle brush to paint the flowers light yellow, occasionally dipping the brush into the dark yellow to add shading. Leave a little bit of white canvas showing in the center of the flower. Let dry. Then paint the leaves light and dark green, using the photograph of the finished rug as a guide. Add a stroke of dark green to the center of each flower, leaving some of the white canvas showing around the green spot. Let dry. TIP: First paint the shapes of the flowers and leaves; then add the darker shade for detail on top.

5 Use the small bristle brush to paint the background around each flower with light and dark green, letting some of the white canvas show between the flowers. Occasionally, dip your brush in the white or black paint and blend these colors with the green paint, allowing the wet areas to blend with each other. This creates a watercolor effect. Let dry. Varnish and wax your floorcloth.

Yellow Roses and Stripes Place Mats

DESIGNER: **RHONDA KAPLAN**

Now that you have yellow roses decorating your floor, why not add them to your table, too! Place mats are an easy way to venture into painting, and these canvas beauties are simple to keep clean. Using the same template and painting techniques as we used on the floorcloth (page 38), you can create place mats to complete a rose theme in your home.

YOU WILL NEED (FOR 4 PLACE MATS)

4 pieces of preprimed canvas, 12 x 16 inches (30 x 40 cm)	Scissors	Small foam paintbrush
Yardstick or ruler	Paints: Light and dark yellow, light and dark green, white, and black	Small artist's paintbrush
Pencil		Varnish
	Paint trays	Paste wax

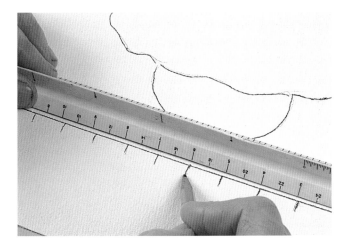

1 Pencil a 2-inch-wide (5 cm) border all around each piece of preprimed canvas. Outline the flower template (see step 2 on page 39) in the center of each place mat. Mark off stripes ¾ inch (1.9 cm) wide all around the border of each place mat.

3 Use the small bristle brush to paint the flower light yellow, occasionally dipping the brush into the dark yellow to add shading. Leave some of the white canvas showing in the center. Let dry. Then paint the leaves light and dark green as shown. Add a stroke of dark green to the center of the flower, leaving some of the white canvas showing around the green spot. Let dry. TIP: First paint the shape of the flower and leaves; then add the darker shade for detail on top.

2 Use the foam brush to paint the stripes light green, and let dry.

4 Use the small bristle brush to paint the background with light and dark green, leaving an area unpainted around the flower. Occasionally dip your brush in the white or black paint and blend these colors with the green paint, allowing the wet areas to blend with each other. This creates a watercolor effect. Let dry. Varnish and wax your place mat.

Twins Roosters

DESIGNER: **JOYCE GARLICK**

Wake up your day with this pair of strutting roosters. This handsome floorcloth is easier to paint than you think. Using simple stenciling, paint pens, and a pattern to trace, you'll soon be crowing with pride over the colorful rug you made yourself!

Hemmed floorcloth, 36 x 48 inches (90 x 120 cm)	Carbon paper	Fine-point artist's paintbrush
Yardstick	Red and green paint pens	Paints: Dark green, orange-red, and grass green
Pencil	Clear plastic stencil film	Paint trays
Painter's masking tape	Scissors	Stencil brush
Tracing paper	Foam or bristle paintbrush	Varnish
		Paste wax

1 Measure and mark a 1¼-inch (3 cm) border from the edge of the canvas. Draw 2-inch (5 cm) corner squares inside the border; then add diagonal lines inside the squares to create triangle shapes. Pencil a wavy line onto all four sides of the floorcloth.

2 Enlarge the rooster design on page 75 as indicated; the circle should measure 16 inches (40 cm) in diameter. Transfer the design twice onto the floorcloth so that the roosters face each other, centered in the middle of the canvas. Place carbon paper under the enlarged drawing, and pencil over all of the lines <u>except</u> for the circle itself.

3 With the green paint pen, paint the wavy lines. Next, with the red paint pen, carefully paint the lines that make up the roosters. Then use dark green paint to fill in the border all around the floor-cloth. Let dry.

4 Using the small artist's brush, paint the red borders around the petals, and let dry. Rinse the brush; then use grass green to paint the petal areas and two of the triangles at the corners. Let dry.

5 Use red paint and the small artist's brush to fill in the other two triangles at the corners. Let dry.

6 Trace the leaf pattern (page 75) onto stencil film, and cut it out. Tape the stencil to the floorcloth along the green wavy line, and use grass green paint and the stencil brush to stencil a leaf. Repeat this process on each side of the four wavy lines, until you have decorated the wavy border with green leaves. Varnish and wax your floorcloth.

Sunflowers and Swirls

DESIGNER: **KATHY COOPER**

Color and images can be powerful tools to lift your mood. Bold, alternating colors are sponged, combed, and swirled onto the canvas to create a floorcloth sure to brighten any room or mood!

YOU WILL NEED

Hemmed floorcloth,
30 x 36 inches (75 x 90 cm)

Painter's masking tape,
2 inches (5 cm) wide

Matte medium

Foam or flat bristle paintbrush

Paint trays

Paints: Blue-green, deep blue, white,
purple, yellow, orange, bright red,
and deep red

Fine-point artist's brush

Rubber combing tool

Round, large sponge pouncer

Varnish

Paste wax

1 Create five large stripes to paint by running off four lines of masking tape evenly spaced across the length of rug. Seal the tape with matte medium, and let dry. You'll be painting the wide stripes with a dry brush mixing technique to variegate the colors (see page 30). First, thin the paint with a small amount of matte medium to make the brushing easier. For the red stripes, mix deep

red and bright red; for the blue stripes, mix a little deep blue and blue-green; for the yellow stripes, mix yellow and orange; for the purple stripes, mix purple and a little white; for the green stripes, mix green and little white. Dip the dry brush into the mixed paints, keeping each color on a separate side of the brush.

2 Brush on the paint, letting the colors blend on the canvas. Paint one stripe at a time in the designated color. Let dry.

3 Remove the tape to expose the thin stripes you'll be painting next. Paint the thin stripes, using the same colors, alternated as shown in the finished rug. Thin the paint first with matte medium. While each thin stripe is wet, pull the rubber combing tool down it. Continue working in this way until all the thin stripes are painted and combed. Be sure to rinse off the comb before moving on to the next stripe. Let dry.

4 Use the fine-point artist's brush to paint three large swirls on the first, third, and fifth wide stripes using three of the same colors as the stripes. TIP: If hand painting swirls seems uncomfortable, you can purchase a swirl stamp at most craft-supply stores.

5 Use chalk to lightly sketch the shape and position of the four sunflowers you'll be painting on the green and purple stripes. Using a flat bristle brush and the dry brush mixing technique, paint the petals on the purple stripe with blue mixed with white, and the petals on the green stripe with red mixed with yellow. Let dry. Paint the center of the blue flowers using red mixed with a little yellow, and the center of the red flowers using yellow mixed with a little red. Use the pouncer to paint the centers by dipping one side of the foam in one color and the other end in the other color; then turn the pouncer slightly while you stamp. Paint dots randomly on each strip, using the colors shown on the finished rug, and let dry. Varnish and wax your floorcloth.

Seeing Spots Place Mats

DESIGNER: **RHONDA KAPLAN**

These place mats look great with the borders painted in different bright colors or in all one color to match the color scheme of your dining area. They're also incredibly easy to paint!

1 Pencil a 3-inch-wide (7.5 cm) border around the edge of the unhemmed, preprimed canvas. (TIP: You can vary the border width to create a more whimsical look.) Pencil spots in the center field, varying the sizes, as shown.

3 Paint the spots black using the round artist's brush, and let dry.

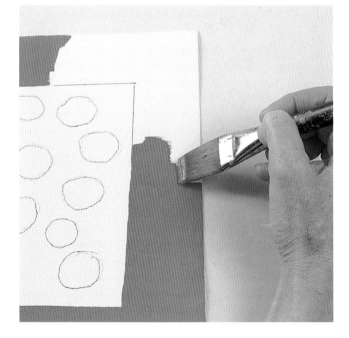

2 Use the small brush to paint the border red or in a variety of other colors. Let dry.

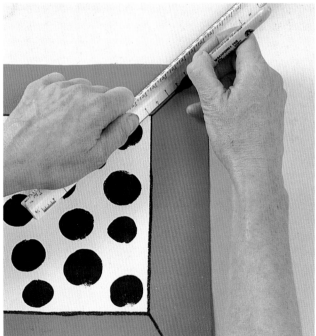

4 Use a yardstick or ruler and the paint pen or marker to outline the border and create diagonal lines in the corners. Let dry. Varnish and wax your place mats.

Combed Checkerboard

DESIGNER: **KATHY COOPER**

A checkerboard grid combined with a combed pattern create this simple but stylish design, reminiscent of older floorcloths. The secret to the pattern is to let each square develop its own colorful and textured characteristics.

YOU WILL NEED

Hemmed floorcloth, 30 x 36 inches (75 x 90 cm)

Pencil

Yardstick

Painter's masking tape

Soft bristle paintbrush

Matte medium

Paint trays

Paints: Yellow ocher, black, and mustard brown

Foam or stiff-bristle paintbrush

Paint conditioner

Rubber combing tool

Varnish

Paste wax

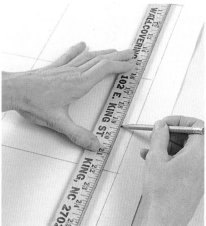

1 Find the center point of the hemmed floorcloth, and mark a grid of 6-inch (15 cm) squares;

there will be four squares top to bottom, and five squares left to right. Mark a 1½-inch (3.75 cm) border from the outside edge. A small ½-inch (1.3 cm) border of squares will fill in the gap.

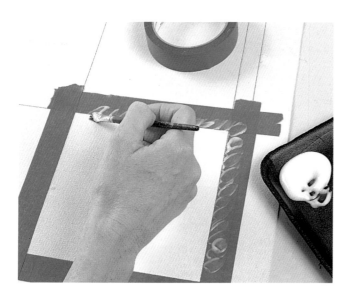

2 Tape around one square, and seal with matte medium. Let dry.

3 Load a paint tray with some yellow ocher, black, and mustard brown; then add a little paint conditioner to thin the paint. Using the dry brush mixing technique (see page 30), lightly dip the foam brush first into each color and then into the paint conditioner; then paint the square. Don't worry about the paint appearing unmixed.

4 While the paint is still wet, place the rubber combing tool at the top of the painted square and pull it through the paint in one direction. (TIP: Practice with the combing tool and the paint on a scrap of canvas or paper to get the feel for how much pressure to apply.) Let dry. Tape the adjacent square, seal the tape, and let dry. Then paint the square, using the same mixing technique. Don't worry if the color of this square is lighter or darker than the one you just completed. In fact, variation is what makes this design so appealing. While the paint is still wet, pull the rubber combing tool in the opposite direction as the adjacent square. This will create a basketweave effect. Let dry. Continue painting and combing squares until you have completed all the full squares and the partial squares along the outside edge. Let dry.

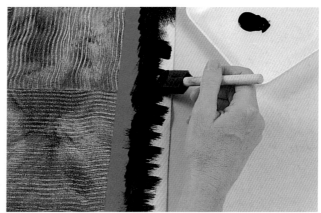

5 After all the squares are painted, run tape along the inside edge of the border, and paint the border black. Let dry. Remove the tape. Varnish and wax your floorcloth.

King and Queen Table Runner

DESIGNER: **FRAN RUBENSTEIN**

Table runners can add color and personality to a dining table or sideboard. Why not let friends and family see who the real lords of the manor are? Using sponge painting, easy-to-copy templates, and free-form hand painting, you can create this delightfully cartoonlike decoration.

YOU WILL NEED

Unhemmed, primed canvas, 11 x 14 inches (28 x 35.5 cm)	Foam or bristle paintbrush	Carbon paper
	Yardstick	Fine-point artist's paintbrush
Paints: Thalo green, white, yellow, red, purple, orange, black, and rose	Pencil	Black paint pen (optional)
	Household sponge	Varnish
Paint trays	Tracing paper	Paste wax

3 Using the artist's brush and yellow paint, color in the two crowns.

1 Paint the unhemmed and primed canvas pale green, and let dry. Measure and mark the two areas for the king and queen on each end. Use a soft household sponge to stamp blue paint on the center portion of the canvas.

4 Use light, carefree strokes to paint the faces as shown in the photograph on page 50. Paint the pink flowers and leaves. Let dry.

2 Make two enlargements of the drawing of the king (page 75) as indicated. This drawing serves for the queen by replacing the straight hair with curls, eliminating the moustache, and giving her a slight nose job! Trace over the copies with tracing paper, and transfer the images to each end of the runner with carbon paper. Enlarge the flower (page 75) to the size indicated, and transfer it repeatedly onto the sponged area with carbon paper, using the photograph of the finished runner as a guide.

5 With the artist's brush and black paint, lightly outline the flowers, the details of the faces, the crown, and the "frame" around the faces. Let dry. (TIP: You can also use a black paint pen for the outlining.) Dip the edge of the sponge in black paint, and run a thin line of paint along the outside edge of the runner. Let dry. Varnish and wax your floorcloth.

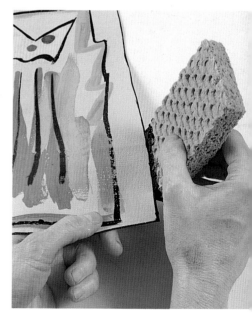

Tasseled Harlequin

DESIGNER: **KATHY COOPER**

This little tasseled beauty could be just the right accent in a small powder room or study. Painted in turquoise green diamonds on a bright blue background and accented with paint pens, it offers royal style on a small scale.

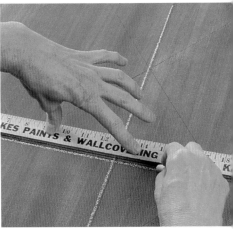

1 Use the foam brush to paint the hemmed floorcloth bright blue, and let dry. Find the center point of the floorcloth by measuring the center of each side and chalking a line that crosses the center. See page 24 for details.

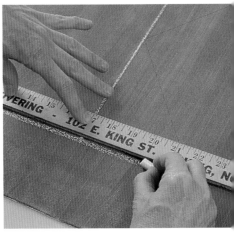

2 Measure off the center point, establishing four rectangle quadrants that are 10 inches (25 cm) wide and 12 inches (30 cm) long.

YOU WILL NEED

Hemmed floorcloth, 31 x 26 inches (77.5 x 65 cm)	White chalk
	Yardstick
Foam paintbrush	Fine-point artist's paintbrush
Paints: Blue, turquoise green, white, and bright red	Gold and black paint pens
	Varnish
Paint tray	Paste wax

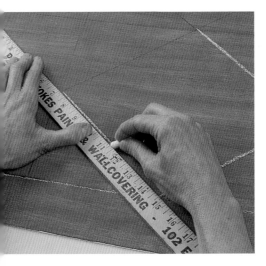

3 Establish the center point on each line of each rectangle.

make the color stand out. If you want, you can tape the areas before you paint them in. Let dry. TIP: Don't worry if the mixed color looks streaky, as this will give the shapes more depth.

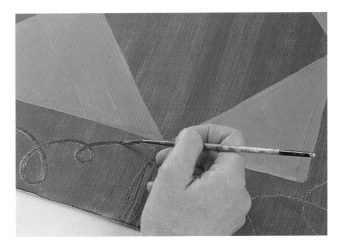

4 Use your yardstick to connect those points, creating squares and triangles.

6 Sketch the tassels and loops with chalk, positioning the tassels at the points of the blue squares. Use the fine-point brush to paint a bright red dot at each of these points; then use the small brush to add red lines, which create the tassel shape. Let dry. Paint the looping lines bright red, and let dry.

7 Outline the field of squares and triangles with a gold paint pen. Use the gold and black paint pens to add highlights to the tassels. Let dry. Varnish and wax your floorcloth.

5 Paint the center square and all the triangles turquoise green, mixing in a little white paint to

Leopard Spots

DESIGNER: **KATHY COOPER**

This faux animal skin looks sensational in any room. Using an easy paint blending technique, some vegetables for stamping, and a few feathered strokes with a brush, you can create this endangered species on canvas.

YOU WILL NEED

Hemmed floorcloth, 30 x 36 inches (75 x 90 cm)

Paint trays

Three foam paintbrushes

Paint conditioner

Paints: mustard brown, medium beige, light beige, black, and clay red

Raw carrot

Raw potato or apple

Sharp knife

Small round bristle paintbrush

Flat bristle paintbrush

China bristle brush or stencil brush

Painter's masking tape

Yardstick

Pencil

Varnish

Paste wax

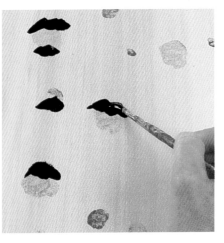

1 Put a small amount of mustard brown, medium beige, and light beige, along with a small amount of paint conditioner, in three paint trays—one color to a tray. For each color, use a clean foam brush. To create the background, start by painting two wide stripes of mustard brown evenly spaced on the floorcloth. Next, brush the medium beige on each side of the mustard brown stripes. Allow the colors to mix slightly and blend; this is a good example of wet-on-wet blending, described on page 30. Repeat this process with light beige, filling in the center and outside edges. Again let the colors blend. You can go back to each color with the original foam brush and blend back and forth until you achieve the desired effect.

3 With the small round brush, randomly dab black spots on the stripes. Working in small sections, outline the dark brown spots with black paint.

4 While the black paint is wet, take a dry China bristle brush or a stencil brush and gently brush the paint to feather it and create the look of hair. Continue working in small sections until you have feathered all of the spots. Let dry.

2 Cut the end off a carrot and dip it into the mustard brown, mixed with a little black. Stamp small spots on the background. Cut a potato or apple into a few small circles that you can hold. Dip the piece of apple or potato into the mixed dark brown paint, and randomly stamp large spots on the background. Continue stamping with the large and small vegetables until you've decorated the stripes to your satisfaction. Let dry.

5 Mark a ¾-inch (1.9 cm) border all around the edge of the floorcloth, and tape it. Use the clay red paint to create a thin stripe around the floorcloth. Let dry. Varnish and wax your floorcloth.

Fish and Dots

DESIGNER: **JOANNA BRITT**

With these fun fish swimming around, you may be inspired to spend more time at the lake or beach! Placed near a bathtub, this colorful, easy-to-paint floorcloth will put anyone in the mood for a dunk.

YOU WILL NEED

Hemmed floorcloth,
24 x 36 inches
(60 x 90 cm)

Yardstick

Pencil

Painter's masking tape

Small foam paintbrush

Paints: Deep purple,
tangerine, olive green,
bright pink, and white

Paint trays

Scissors

White chalk

Small artist's bristle paintbrush

Small foam pouncer

White and black paint pens

Varnish

Paste wax

1 Measure 6 inches (15 cm) from the edge of the hemmed floorcloth, and mark the border. Run masking tape along the bottom of the pencil line. Seal with white paint, and let dry.

3 Enlarge the fish (page 76) to the size indicated. Cut out the fish template. Using the photograph of the finished rug as a guide for placement, outline the fish with white chalk along the border. Use the small artist's brush to paint the fish orange, and let dry.

4 Use the foam pouncer and the green paint to stamp dots in the center of the floorcloth. Let dry.

2 Use the foam brush to paint the area inside the taped border pink and the area outside the taped border purple. Let dry. Remove the tape.

5 Use the black paint pen to add details to the fish. Use the white paint pen to outline the dots and the fish. Varnish and wax your floorcloth.

Watering Cans

DESIGNER: **JOYCE GARLICK**

Gardening and flowers are popular motifs for floorcloth designers. Using a template, paint pens, and simple painting techniques, you can create this appealing design, sure to shed a lot of sunshine in your own mudroom or foyer.

YOU WILL NEED

Hemmed floorcloth,
36 x 42 inches
(90 x 105 cm)

Yardstick

Pencil

Painter's masking tape

Matte medium

Foam paintbrush

Paints: Light yellow, light green,
and dark green

Paint trays

Soft bristle paintbrush

Tracing paper

Carbon paper

Dark green paint pen

Fine-point artist's paintbrush

Varnish

Paste wax

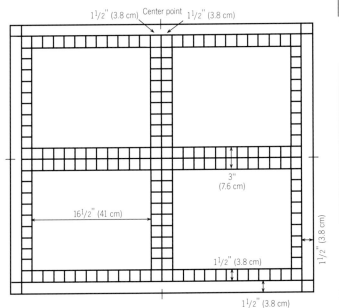

1½" (3.8 cm) Center point 1½" (3.8 cm)

16½" (41 cm)

3"
(7.6 cm)

1½" (3.8 cm)

1½" (3.8 cm)

1½" (3.8 cm)

1 Measure and mark two borders each 1½ inches (3.8 cm) wide, running along the outer edges of the rug. Measure the center point on each side of the floorcloth and connect the points to create a large cross. Mark a row 1½ inches (3.8 cm) wide on both sides of this cross.

3 Tape off the alternating rectangles. Seal with matte medium, and let dry. Paint the yellow and green rectangles, and let dry. Tape off the outside border of the floorcloth. Seal with matte medium, and let dry. Paint the border yellow, and let dry. Remove all the tape.

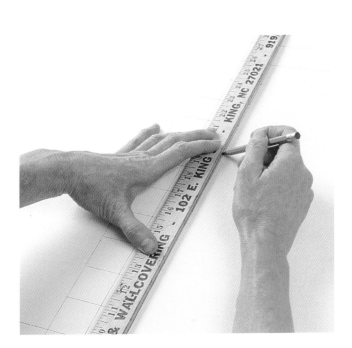

2 Mark checks 1½ inches (3.8 cm) wide on all borders, except the one closest to the edge of the floorcloth, as shown in step 1.

4 Enlarge the watering can (page 74) to the size indicated. Place carbon paper under the enlarged template, and pencil over the lines to transfer the watering can onto the floorcloth. Refer to the finished floorcloth for placement of the watering cans.

5 On the yellow rectangles, paint the watering cans green; on the green rectangles, paint the watering cans yellow. Let dry.

7 Use the fine-point artist's brush to paint the alternating checks dark green, and let dry. Paint the outside corners dark green, and let dry. Varnish and wax your floorcloth.

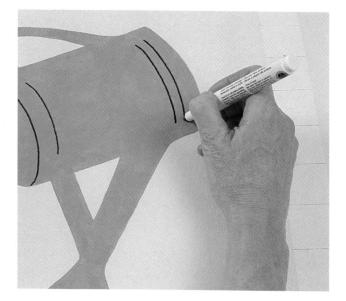

6 Outline the watering cans with the green paint pen.

Diamond and Tassel Valance

DESIGNERS: **MICEY MOYER AND POLLY EAGAN**

If you can't find the right fabric to sew a valance that matches your decor
(or if you just don't sew!), you can paint one using floorcloth canvas.
Armed with gold tassels, foam stamps, and simple brush strokes, you can
create a lovely valance or two in a weekend.

YOU WILL NEED (FOR EACH VALANCE)

Unhemmed primed canvas,
33 x 18 inches
(85 x 45 cm)

Yardstick

Pencil

Heavyweight, self-stick
hook-and-loop tape

Paints: Black, raw umber, white, and
metallic gold

Paint trays

Foam paintbrushes

Small bristle artist's paintbrush

Sharp scissors

Spiral rubber stamp

2 gold tassels

Craft glue optional

Curtain rod

Varnish

Paste wax

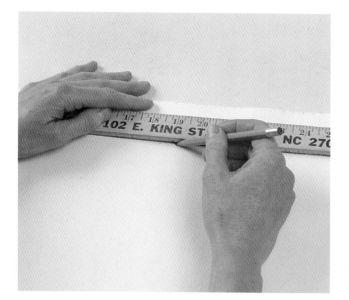

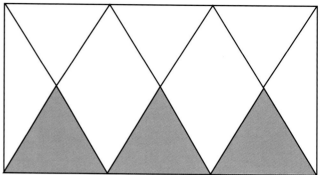

3 Measure the diamonds by dividing the long side of the canvas into thirds. Mark the top and bottom of the valance, and connect lines to form two full and two half diamonds on the sides, and three half diamonds on the top and bottom, as shown in the drawing.

1 On the front side of the primed canvas, measure and mark a 2-inch (5 cm) border across one long side; this will create a rod pocket at the top of the valance. Fold the border toward the back side of the canvas.

2 Turn the canvas over, and adhere four or five 3-inch (7.5 cm) strips of hook-and-loop tape to the folded over border and the canvas where the border meets.

4 Paint the two half diamonds on the side, and the half diamond on the top center black. Let dry.

5 Mix some raw umber and white paint to create a rich gray. Define all the diamond shapes by painting the outlines of the insides of the diamonds gray. (TIP: To create subtle shading, use the dry brush mixing technique described on page 30.) Let dry.

7 Paint metallic gold paint onto the spiral rubber stamp, and stamp spirals on some of the diamonds.

6 Cut away the three half diamonds on the bottom row (the shaded areas in the drawing with step 3).

8 Use the artist's brush and the gray paint to add shadow details on the diamonds. If you want, you can also add additional shadows with gold paint. Let dry. Varnish and wax your valance. Glue the gold tassels onto the bottom points of the valance.

Big B Baby Floorcloth

DESIGNER: **DEBBY FREEMAN**

Designed to lay under your child's high chair, this fun and colorful floorcloth will delight your enthusiastic "B-for-Baby" eater, and catch flying food, too! With templates, simple painting, and paint pens, it's easy to replicate this practical spill catcher. You can also personalize it with H for Happy Hannah or S for Sloppy Sam.

YOU WILL NEED

Hemmed floorcloth, 40 x 40 inches (100 x 100 cm)

Yardstick

Pencil

Round object, such as a bowl or plastic lid, about 8 inches (20 cm) wide

Foam paintbrushes

Artist's small bristle paintbrush

Paints: Light orange, dark orange, yellow, black, purple, grass green, magenta, turquoise, and white

Paint trays

Letter template*

Carbon paper

Black paint pen or permanent marker

Varnish

Paste wax

*Craft-supply stores sell templates and stencils for letters.

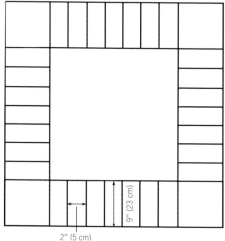

2" (5 cm)   9" (23 cm)

1 Pencil a 9-inch (23 cm) border all around the canvas. Mark 2-inch-wide (5 cm) stripes on the border areas, leaving the four corners empty.

2 Outline the round object with pencil to create 8-inch (20 cm) diameter circles in the corners.

3 Use a brush to paint the center field pale yellow, and let dry. Lightly mix the yellow and the orange in the paint tray, and paint in the orange circles, using the artist's brush. Let dry.

4 Use a brush to paint the stripes blue and green. Let dry. TIP: Don't try to make the stripes exact; here and there, leave little white spaces between the stripes.

5 Enlarge the letter B on a copier (see page 76) to the size indicated, or use a template for the letter of your choice. Cut out the letter, and transfer it onto the center of the floorcloth with carbon paper. Enlarge the bug on a copier (see page 76) to the size indicated, cut it out, and transfer the image onto the rug with carbon paper. Refer to the finished floor-cloth for placement. Paint the letter black with the detail brush.

6 Paint the bugs white, and let dry. Then paint the bugs assorted colors, using the photograph as a guide. Let dry. Outline the bug shapes with black paint pen or marker, and let dry. Varnish and wax your floorcloth.

Tapestry Border

DESIGNER: **VIRGINIA STOVALL**

The rich look of tapestry has become popular again, and this rug makes use of a commercial fabric border framing a simple faux finish floorcloth. Using simple rag rolling and basic sewing skills, you'll be able to create a stunning accent for your home.

YOU WILL NEED

Unhemmed preprimed canvas, 24 x 30 inches (60 x 75 cm)

Foam or bristle paintbrush

Paints: Sage green and dark sage green

Large bowl or small bucket

Paint conditioner

Soft rag

Yardstick

Pencil

4 yards (3.7 m) of 8-inch-wide (20 cm) tapestry fabric

Sewing machine

Contact cement

Varnish

Paste wax

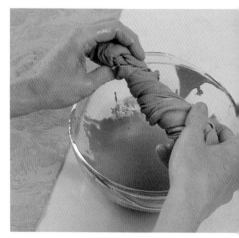

1 Paint the unhemmed preprimed canvas light sage green, and let dry. In the bowl or bucket, pour in one part dark green paint, one part paint conditioner, and a little less than one part water. Wet the rag in water and wring it out completely. Keep the rag twisted, dip it in the glaze, and squeeze out the excess.

2 Tuck in the ends of the rag, and roll the rag over the entire surface of the floorcloth, using the rag like a paint roller. Let dry.

3 Mark a 5-inch (12.5 cm) border all around the canvas. Sew the tapestry border face down to the left of the marked border on all four sides of the canvas, leaving the excess at each end.

4 Fold the mitered corners on each end, and trim the excess tapestry, leaving a small amount for the seam allowance.

5 Glue the folded, mitered corners with contact cement.

6 Fold the outer edges of the tapestry border and glue them to the back of the tapestry. Varnish and wax your floorcloth, taking care to apply these materials only on the painted surface.

Southwest Borders

DESIGNER: **MAGGIE VALE**

For an attractive Southwestern decorating accent, you can make this easy rug
featuring seven borders. All you need are some homemade sponge stamps, a
little hand painting, and a love of desert colors.

YOU WILL NEED

Hemmed floorcloth, 24 x 36 inches (60 x 90 cm)	Paint trays	Matte medium (optional)
	Yardstick	Household sponge
Paints: Green, red, yellow, teal, black, purple, white, and terra cotta	Pencil	Scissors
	Small soft bristle paintbrush	Varnish
Foam or bristle paintbrush	Painter's masking tape (optional)	Paste wax

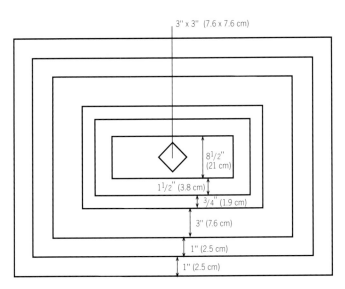

3" x 3" (7.6 x 7.6 cm)

8¹/₂" (21 cm)

1¹/₂" (3.8 cm)

³/₄" (1.9 cm)

3" (7.6 cm)

1" (2.5 cm)

1" (2.5 cm)

4 Cut a small triangle from the sponge. Dip it in the purple paint, and stamp triangles inside the green and red borders. Let dry.

1 Paint the hemmed floorcloth terra cotta, and let dry. Measure and mark five borders, as shown in the drawing. Measure the center point of the entire floorcloth, and pencil a square 3 x 3 inches (7.6 x 7.6 cm) in size.

5 Cut two small squares from the sponge. Dip one in the black paint and stamp black squares inside the yellow wavy border and the green border. Outline four squares with black paint inside the center square. Stamp two of the squares black. Dip the other square sponge in white paint, and stamp the other two squares white. Let dry.

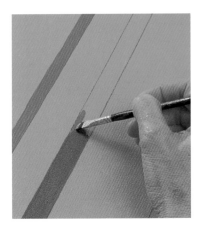

2 Use the artist's brush to paint the borders and the outline of the small centered square, using the photograph of the finished rug as a guide for color placement. (TIP: You can tape around each penciled line and seal with matte medium, if you're uncomfortable hand painting. Painter's masking tape will easily pull off the painted surface.)

3 Pencil a curved line around the inside of the 3-inch (7.6 cm) border, and paint the line yellow. Let dry.

6 Dip the eraser end of the pencil in the blue paint, and randomly stamp blue dots on the wavy border. Rinse off the eraser. Dip it in the white paint, and randomly stamp white dots on the blue triangles. Let dry. Varnish and wax your floorcloth.

Starry Night

DESIGNER: **FRANCIE RILEY**

Drift among the stars every day when you step on this floorcloth! Using an easy wet paint blending technique, foam stamps, and spatter paint, you will count your lucky stars to have created this lovely rug. We like the floorcloth so much we displayed it on the wall…easy to do by adding a rod pocket (see page 62).

YOU WILL NEED

Hemmed floorcloth,
29 x 50 inches
(73 x 125 cm)

Paints: Black, dark blue,
and metallic gold

Paint trays

Foam or bristle paintbrush

Packing foam

Scissors

Paint conditioner

Old paintbrush

Varnish

Paste wax

1 Brush black paint randomly over the entire floorcloth, leaving some of the white canvas showing.

3 Cut the packing foam into the shapes of stars and spirals. Dip the cut foam in gold paint, and stamp gold stars and spirals in a random pattern over the entire background. Let dry.

2 While the paint is still wet, brush dark blue paint over the white areas and allow the paint to blend. TIP: Vary the direction of the brush strokes to achieve a rich and vibrant effect. Let dry.

4 Load an old, preferably, splayed, paintbrush with gold paint. Thin the gold paint with a small amount of paint conditioner. Spatter the paint from each side of the floorcloth to get even coverage. Before flicking your brush, look around you to make sure you won't spatter anything or anyone else! Let dry. Varnish and wax your floorcloth.

Amish Quilt

DESIGNER: **FRANCIE RILEY**

Simple geometry and subtle colors make this Amish quilt pattern a handsome accent to any room. Using a dry brush mixing technique and a paint pen, this floorcloth is easy to duplicate.

YOU WILL NEED

Hemmed floorcloth, 29 x 50 inches (73 x 125 cm)

Yardstick

Pencil

Painter's masking tape

Foam or flat-bristle paintbrushes

Paint trays

Gold paint pen

Paints: Yellow ocher, moss green, and white

Varnish

Paste wax

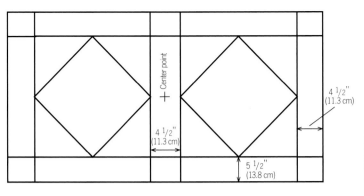

streaky effect. In the corners, use the brush to make circular strokes. Let dry. TIP: Brush the paint directionally around the geometric pattern. Don't worry about bleeds under the tape; the gold paint pen will help to conceal this later.

1 Mark the quilt design on the hemmed floorcloth, using a yardstick and pencil. First measure a 4½-inch (11.3 cm) border on the ends and a 5½-inch (13.8 cm) border down the long sides, allowing the corners to crisscross. Next, measure the center of the canvas, and mark a 4½-inch (11.3 cm) border straddling the center point.

4 Tape off all the areas to be painted ocher. First brush on the ocher. Then, use the same dry brush mixing technique to work the ocher and white together on the canvas to create a streaky effect. In the center of the squares, create a circular brush pattern. Let dry.

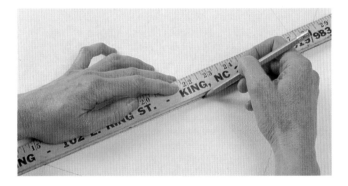

2 Create a small square on its end inside each of the large squares by marking a center point on each side of the large square and then connecting the lines, as shown in the drawing with step 1.

3 Tape off all the areas to be painted green. Brush on the green and white paint together, using the dry brush mixing technique (see page 30), to create a

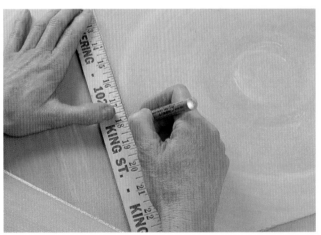

5 Use the yardstick and the gold paint pen to outline the ocher areas. Let dry. Varnish and wax your floorcloth.

TEMPLATES

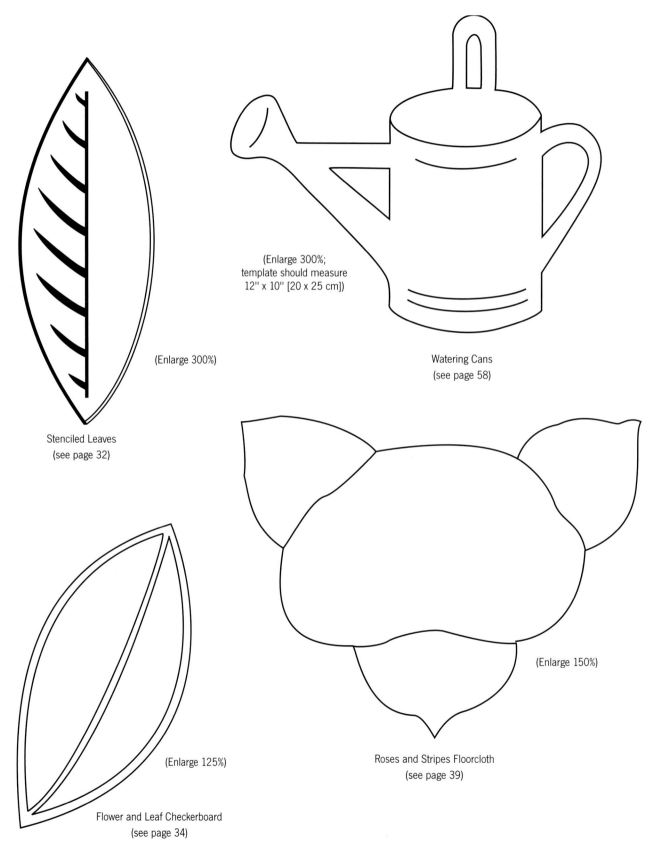

(Enlarge 300%)

Stenciled Leaves
(see page 32)

(Enlarge 300%;
template should measure
12" x 10" [20 x 25 cm])

Watering Cans
(see page 58)

(Enlarge 125%)

Flower and Leaf Checkerboard
(see page 34)

(Enlarge 150%)

Roses and Stripes Floorcloth
(see page 39)

(Enlarge 400%;
circle should measure
16" [40 cm] in diameter)

(100%)

Twin Roosters
(see page 42)

(Enlarge 150%)

King and Queen Table Runner
(see page 50)

(Enlarge 300%; template should measure
12½" x 12½" [31 cm])

(Enlarge 150%)

Fish and Dots
(see page 56)

(Enlarge 250%)

(Enlarge 350%;
template should measure
13" x 9" [32.5 x 23 cm])

Big B Baby Floorcloth
(see page 64)

ABOUT THE AUTHOR

KATHY COOPER has been a full-time floorcloth artist since 1979, producing one-of-a-kind and custom work for interior designers and clients. She presents workshops and lectures on floorcloth design and construction, and has been a featured guest on national television, promoting her first book *The Complete Book of Floorcloths* (Lark Books,1997). She can be reached at: Orchard House Floorcloths, 1953 Covington Road, King, NC 27021, 336-994-2612, e-mail floorcloths@hotmail.com http://www.kathycooperfloorcloths.com.

ABOUT THE DESIGNERS

JOANNA BRITT is an artist of many persuasions, including watercolor, pastels, and floorcloths. She has illustrated and written children's stories. She teaches art at the Sawtooth Center for Visual Art in her hometown of Winston-Salem, North Carolina. She has been making floorcloths since 1994. She can be reached at: 3870 Will Scarlet Rd, Winston-Salem, NC 27104, 336-768-1776, e-mail Wilnoady@msn.com.

DEBBY FREEMAN capitalized on her experience in public relations to market her own business, painting furniture and canvas. She has been making floorcloths since 1989, and markets her whimsical custom designs to local clients. She can be reached at: 945 Jamestown Crescent, Norfolk, VA 23508, 757-451-2275.

JOYCE GARLICK turned to floorcloths in 1993 as a way to combine her background in graphics and her interest in interior design. She is a full-time floorcloth artist, and markets her work through designers and specialty shops. She can be reached at: Joyce Garlick Designs, 9129 Rich Woods Court, Loveland, OH 45140, 513-683-9571.

RHONDA KAPLAN has been making floorcloths since 1990. Her background in commercial art and children's clothing gives her work a contemporary, colorful look. She markets her floorcloths and place mats through fine craft shows and retail stores. She can be reached at: East Lake Designs, 119 East Lake Drive, Annapolis, MD 21403, 410-268-5989, e-mail Eastlake@AOL.com

MICEY MOYER AND POLLY EAGAN have been making floorcloths since 1994. Micey, a former children's clothing shop owner and floral designer, and Polly, a realtor, turned to floorcloths as a creative outlet. They produce limited custom work for local clients from their warehouse studio in the popular downtown art district. They can be reached at: Micey Moyer/Polly Eagan, Floorcloth Designs Inc, 228 Hollywood Drive, Metarie, LA 70005, 504-588-9200.

FRANCIE RILEY began making floorcloths for the theater industry. She painted floorcloths for many different sets, and began to produce floorcloths to sell full-time in 1987. She markets her custom work through interior designers. She can be reached at: Riley Design, #3 Lee Rd, Croton Falls, NY 10519, 914-277-0860 , e-mail rileydesign@webtv.net.

FRAN RUBENSTEIN has been making floorcloths since 1981. With a background in fabric and wallpaper design, she began making floorcloths because of the flexibility of design for the floor. She is a full-time floorcloth artist, and sells her work through fine craft shows, interior designers, and retail stores. She can be reached at: Divine Inspirations, 1350 14th Ave, Grafton, WI 53024. 414-375-9876, e-mail franfromwi@webtv.net.

VIRGINIA STOVALL is an artist with an interest in interior design, who fell in love with floorcloths after reading *The Complete Book of Floorcloths*. She has worked extensively in the decorative accessories field, and has been making custom floorcloths since 1997. Her work is available at her store This and That Imports. She can be reached at: Virginia Stovall Designs, 7257 Meadowbrook Dr, Mandeville. LA 70741, 504-624-3364, e-mail VSto885154@AOL.com.

MAGGIE VALE has been making floorcloths since 1989. While working as a boat captain, delivering classic wooden sailboats with canvas sails, she fell in love with canvas. She is a full-time floorcloth artist, and sells her floorcloths through design centers or by commission. She can be reached at: Maggie Vale Floorcloths, 15 Bayside Ave, Newport, RI 02840, 401-846-4245, e-mail maggieevale@hotmail.com.

SOURCES FOR FLOORCLOTH SUPPLIES

Canvas and Paints

Fredrix Artist Canvas
Box 646
111 Fredrix Alley
Lawrenceville, GA 30246-0646
(800) 241-8129
Wide selection of canvas, both primed and unprimed;
call for a retailer near you.

Lakearts
PO Box 1285
Flowery Branch, GA 30542
(888) 464-2787
www.lakearts.com
Wide selection of floorcloth supplies, including
canvas, acrylic finish, double-stick hem tape,
and paints

Utrecht
133 35th Street
Brooklyn, NY 11232
1-800-223-9132
www.utrechtart.com
Wide selection of floorcloth supplies, including
canvas, paints, matte medium, gesso, acrylic
varnish, and paintbrushes

Jerry's Artarama
PO Box 1105
New Hyde Park, NY 11040
(800) U-ARTIST
www.jerryscatalog.com
Offers canvas, paints, matte medium, paintbrushes,
and other art supplies

Paste Wax

Na-Nor Bowling Alley Wax
C.A. Nash & Sons Inc.
Att: Ridgely Nash
PO Box 6226
Norfolk, VA 23508
1-757-622-5651
Family run business selling transparent white paste
wax; leave a message with name and phone number
for order information.

Canada

All Weather Canvas Products
2 Thornecliffe Park Drive, Unit #35
Toronto, Ontario M4H 1H2
(877) 696-9009 Toll free
Sells 5-ft (1.5 m) and 10-ft (3 m) widths of canvas

Woolfitts Art Enterprises, Inc
1153 Queen Street, W
Toronto, Ontario M6J 1J4
(800) 490-3567
Retail store and wholesale catalog, featuring canvas,
acrylic paints, varnish, and other art supplies

THANKS!

Writing a book is a glamorous job that requires many "unglamorous" tasks! To help pull all of the parts together I called on many sources, and each one kept me going. I would like to thank and acknowledge the support of:

Rob Pulleyn, who believed I had another book in me.

Carol Taylor, who took me down the path to an editor, and gave me permission to go to Greece and have a great time!

Deborah Morgenthal, the editor and details person, who kept all the parts together, and reassured me professionally and personally.

Kathy Holmes, the art director, who makes the visual image come together so wonderfully.

Evan Bracken, the photographer, who is so patient and observant and easy to work with.

Ashely Siegel, who welcomed us into her beautiful home so that we could photograph floorcloths.

Fredrix Artist Canvas for supplying the canvas for the projects, and Pete Delin for his continued support.

Joanna Britt, Debby Freeman, Joyce Garlick, Rhonda Kaplan, Micey Moyer, Polly Eagan, Francie Riley, Fran Rubenstein, Virginia Stovall, and Maggie Vale, who all took time out of their busy schedules to make projects for the book, and were willing to share their own designs and ideas.

My friends and family, who always believe I can do it.

My beautiful daughters, Sunny and Libba, who remind me everyday that life is a wonderful adventure.

INDEX